"When I realized you and your family . . . killed by the buffalo, I was so scared I would have bet I'd never laugh again."

Wyatt heard more in her voice than the worry of a rancher for her neighbor. He heard the same thing he'd heard that morning two weeks ago when she hadn't liked finding him with Jeanie. The same thing he'd heard behind every insult and apology. There couldn't be anything between them. . .but there was.

Without making a conscious choice, Wyatt reached for her and pulled her into his arms. She looked startled, but she let him drag her over to his side of the truck.

Wyatt, knowing every move was pure stupid, lowered his head.

Lights in the rearview mirror jerked them apart.

Buffy scooted away from him so quickly, Wyatt thought she'd been snagged by a lasso and hog-tied to her door.

MARY CONNEALY is an author, journalist, and teacher. She writes for three divisions of Barbour Publishing: Heartsong Presents, Barbour Trade Fiction, and Heartsong Presents Mysteries. Mary lives on a farm in Nebraska with her husband, Ivan. They have four daughters: Joslyn—married to Matt; Wendy; Shelly—married to Aaron; and Katy.

Books by Mary Connealy

HEARTSONG PRESENTS
HP744—Golden Days

Buffalo
Gal

Mary Connealy

Heartsong Presents

Two people are really responsible (or to blame) for me writing. Wendy Connealy and Janell Gatewood Carson. Wendy, my daughter, was ten or eleven when she wrote this very short book about the Bermuda Triangle, and it was really good. I'm still in negotiations with her to steal her idea. So far. . .no way. Janell, my kindergarten classmate, interviewed all the WWII veterans in her area (not while she was *in* kindergarten) and got a book printed to sell in the local county museum. It was really well done and a fun, fascinating read. I was so impressed with both of them and thought, *If they can write a book, maybe I can, too,* and fired up my computer for the first time. Thank you both for being an inspiration.

A note from the Author:
I love to hear from my readers! You may correspond with me by writing:

Mary Connealy
Author Relations
PO Box 721
Uhrichsville, OH 44683

ISBN 978-1-60260-077-5

BUFFALO GAL

Our mission is to publish and distribute inspirational products offering exceptional value and biblical encouragement to the masses.

PRINTED IN THE U.S.A.

one

Buffy Lange had been at her new job for fifteen minutes. It was going to take a miracle to last out the hour.

"Don't let him through that gate!" She sprinted toward the fence.

The buffalo hit the metal panel with a clang of horns on steel. A dozen wranglers started shouting and rushing to support the slipping barrier between a buffalo and freedom. The young bull stubbornly refused to pass through the alleyway of metal panels. The massive brute swung his head, snapping a hinge holding the gate in place.

Buffy, coming from inside another pen, grabbed the top of the fence, vaulted it, and beat the wranglers to the action. Snatching the slipping tubular steel, she shoved her shoulder into it, closing the gap.

Two thousand pounds of cranky bison rammed the wobbling panel.

Her shoulder was no match. Buffy fell backward into the mud with the gate on top of her.

The buffalo's legs tangled in the open spaces of the slatted panel, and it stopped.

With the wind knocked out of her, Buffy looked eye to eye with the frantic animal who snorted hot breath in her face. The bull swung his horns, and adrenaline sizzled through Buffy's veins like an electric current.

The crushing steel gate rang and shuddered from the blow, but it blocked the goring horns. One sharp hoof scraped between Buffy's arm and her stomach. It ripped her sleeve and

5

scraped off some of her hide. One last enraged snort and the beast plunged forward and was gone, its hind legs missing her by inches.

Screams and shouts echoed in the ranch yard.

Buffy prayed for that miracle.

Needing direct intervention from God to keep her hired men alive and herself employed looked bad on a résumé.

The panel wrenched off and hands ran down her arms and legs. She opened her eyes, and Wolf Running Shield, her foreman, crouched over her. His black braids, shot through with gray, slid over both his shoulders and dangled over her head. "Are you okay?" His bottomless ebony eyes flashed with worry. "Did he land a hoof on you?"

Her abused lungs started working, and she dragged in the hot July air. "I'm fine."

"Mommy!" The bloodcurdling scream came from Sally, her three-year-old niece, supposedly confined to the house until the buffalo was safely penned.

Everyone around Buffy vanished, running to the rescue. Buffy jerked her arms out of the mud and scrambled to her feet.

A man, rigged out like a cowboy straight from the old West, raced his horse between the buffalo and Sally.

"Hiyah!" the cowboy shouted and slapped his horse's rump with an open hand. He thundered down on Sally a split second before the buffalo and snagged her by the front of her pink overalls. He swung Sally up in front of him, still at a full gallop.

The buffalo changed course and went after the horse and rider.

"Where's a tranquilizer gun?" Buffy noticed Wolf dashing toward the nearest barn and hoped he was getting one.

The horse headed right toward a cluster of scrambling men gathered to watch the buffalo join the family. The rider, with inches between his horse's heels and the lowered horns of the buffalo, wheeled his mount away from the crowd.

The buffalo's horns hooked at the horse. They missed by a hair breadth.

The cowboy held Sally, still screaming, perched high in front of him. His horse danced away from the charging bull and began zigzagging across the open yard to avoid people. The man moved with his horse like they were one creature.

The shaggy beast lost interest in the horse and rider, whirled away, and charged toward the prairie that surrounded the Buffalo Commons Ranch.

For a split second, the adrenaline and the beauty of the buffalo made Buffy feel like she could fly.

The great shaggy beasts were meant to run free on the boundless South Dakota hills and prairies. But these hills and prairies had bounds, and her buffalo was out of them.

The cowboy yelled again and kicked his horse, galloping toward the ranch house. He set Sally down beside Jeanie. He took two seconds to speak some words to both of them that made Sally fling herself against her mother's legs and Jeanie cross her arms and scowl. He pulled a rifle out of a stock on his saddle. Yelling, he bent low over his saddle horn and took off after the disappearing buffalo, his intentions lethal.

"He's going to shoot Bill." Buffy whirled away from the angry man on his charging horse.

Wolf ran up beside her with the tranquilizer gun. "You drive!"

They dashed for the pickup, hooked up to the trailer that only seconds ago held the prize bull. With quick, efficient motions, Wolf unhooked the stock trailer while Buffy jumped in the driver's seat. Wolf threw himself into the passenger's side. They tore out of the yard and into the grass that stretched for miles in all directions in this fertile valley circled by the peaks of the Black Hills.

The buffalo appeared on a rise then vanished.

"The land seems so flat," Buffy muttered, her foot shoved all the way to the floorboard.

The rider appeared, closing the gap between himself and the buffalo. Buffy lay on her horn, but the rider didn't look back. If anything, he leaned down farther on his horse's neck, trying to get more speed out of the big bay quarter horse.

"It's deceiving. There are low rolling hills right up to the mountains." Wolf loaded the rifle with able efficiency.

"He wants to kill the bull before we get there," Buffy yelled. "I can't believe this. The man can't possibly intend to shoot down an animal as valuable as that buffalo."

"That's Wyatt Shaw," Wolf said, shaking his head. "He's the second-biggest rancher around here, after our boss, Leonard. He hates buffalo, and he hates what we're doing. I think he's been looking for an excuse to put a bullet in a buff ever since we moved the first head onto the ranch."

Shaw raised his gun. There was a sharp *crack* of rifle fire.

The buffalo swerved in a different direction but charged on. He seemed unhurt, but a buffalo could run a long time after it had been wounded.

Buffy tried to coax more speed out of the truck. They roared up the crest of one of the endless swells of land and were airborne as they came over the top and dropped down. They gained on Shaw as Shaw gained on her buffalo. She jammed her foot more firmly on the accelerator.

Shaw took aim. Another report cut her eardrums.

The buffalo swerved sharply, now running at a right angle to Buffy. She cut across the angle, hoping to narrow the gap and get there first. Bill gave her a glance and swerved back the way he'd been going.

The cowboy, still running flat out, turned and glared at her. Even from this distance, she saw straight into hazel eyes that shot sparks of golden fire at her. There was such fury burning there she wondered if her buffalo was the only one in danger.

Shaw looked away and aimed his rifle. He fired.

The buffalo turned. Buffy veered across prairie, trying to cut it off.

Wolf caught her arm. "Don't do that. Keep going straight."

"Why? We can beat Shaw to Bill."

"Do it," Wolf snarled. "Straighten it out."

Buffy didn't like it. She was the boss, had been for almost thirty minutes now. But she needed to keep her eyes on the dipping and rolling prairie. She did as Wolf said just to keep things simple.

Now Shaw and Bill were running at a ninety-degree angle to her. Shaw raised his gun and took careful aim.

Wolf lifted his gun from the cab of the pickup. They were nearly within range.

Shaw fired. The buffalo swerved away from the gunfire.

"It's almost impossible to hit anything from the back of a running horse or the cab of a bouncing truck," Wolf said. "Stop when I say."

"Okay." Buffy gripped the wheel with white knuckles. Her blood pounded until she heard it in her ears and her temples. Her arm burned from Bill's scraping hoof. Her body felt like a time bomb vibrating before it exploded.

Wolf nodded. "Keep going straight. That buff'll keep to the low ground when he gets to that rise."

Shaw almost lay down on the back of his horse and steadied the gun across his arm. He fired. Bill stumbled.

"He hit him," Buffy said through her clenched teeth.

"No, he didn't."

"He's going to kill him before we get there," Buffy raged.

Her truck hit a rut that launched the front end into the air. They landed and bounced, and the underbelly of the truck grated against the ground.

Bill ran steadily, as wild and beautiful as buffalo had been at God's creation.

Buffy tried to gain every second she could, even if it meant her rig was destroyed. That buffalo was more valuable than this shiny, new Ford.

Bill took the low ground, just as Wolf had predicted. That turned him until he was headed almost straight toward them.

Wolf shouted, "Stop!"

Buffy wrestled the rig to a halt, tires skidding on grass.

Wolf leaped out, graceful even with deep wrinkles cutting lines into the corners of his eyes. He braced the tranquilizer gun against the hood of the truck and settled his finger on the trigger.

A whirl of dust caught up with the truck and swallowed them. To Buffy, everything suddenly seemed to be in slow motion. Sitting in the cab, her heart pounded, her nerves screamed, her blood coursed, pushing her to action.

Wolf looked down the barrel of his gun. Bill charged closer, hooves drumming until the prairie shook.

Shaw raced behind Bill, his horse's hooves thundering along with the buffalo.

Wolf sited his gun.

Shaw leveled his rifle. Buffy knew he wanted the buffalo dead.

That's when she remembered to pray. She'd already asked God for a miracle when Sally was in a direct line between Bill and freedom. When she'd prayed, there, instantly—Wyatt Shaw.

This buffalo hater was no answer to her prayers. She stifled her resentment at God. One more thing she needed to control.

Bill closed to within a hundred yards, and still Wolf waited.

Shaw charged behind the bull; he was close enough now that he couldn't miss. Not even on a running horse. Buffy saw his cold fury and shuddered.

Wolf waited, waited. Buffy almost saw Wolf's Native American blood flowing cool and steady in his veins.

The buffalo was a hundred feet away. Then fifty.

Wolf exhaled slowly, held his breath. He fired.

A bright red flag marked the dart's direct hit on Bill's densely furred chest. Bill kept coming, his hooves rolling with the steady beat of distant thunder. His horns gleamed with the sharp danger of lightning. He showed no sign of being drugged.

Wolf held his ground.

"You can't shoot him again," Buffy yelled as she swung her door open. "He can't take that much sedative."

Shaw was almost on top of Bill. He could have leaned forward, and slapped him on the rear end. He leveled his gun forward, and Buffy saw him cock the hammer.

Buffy slammed the truck door and ran to the front of the truck. To protect her bull, she'd tackle Wolf if he decided to shoot again.

Wolf gave her one enraged glance. "Get out of here."

Buffy shouted to Shaw, "Don't shoot him. We've got him under—"

Suddenly Bill was on top of them, and Wolf vanished.

Buffy stumbled backward, bumped into the truck grill, and barely missed those sharp, curved horns. Something tightened on her neck like she was being strangled, and with a speed that made her stomach swoop, she was airborne.

She landed with a *thud* on the hood. Bill turned and smashed his wicked horns into the truck where she'd been.

Wolf had her by the collar. He released her with a look of disgust. "Crazy woman."

Bill whirled away from the truck then charged again. He slammed into the front fender and shook the rig hard enough that Buffy slid sideways to the ground. Bill turned on her.

Shaw's horse burst past the buffalo, and he gripped the front of her shirt in both his fists. As if she weighed nothing, he hoisted her into the air and set her down facing him, her legs straddling his saddle, her face pressed against his chest. He set his horse to dancing and dodging just as he'd done with Sally.

Wolf yelled, "It'll take affect in another couple of minutes, Wyatt."

Shaw said, with a rage so icy it chilled the back of Buffy's neck, "Great. I've got nothing better to do than keep this fool woman alive."

Buffy glanced up at the man who'd just saved her life. While Shaw was freezing her with his voice, he was burning her with his eyes. Buffy's head was spinning from the pivoting of the horse and the snorting of the grouchy buffalo and, just maybe, from the scent of a strong man wrapped in leather and sweat and rage, holding her.

For one second, she felt safe. She tightened her arms around Wyatt's waist and held on tight as she wondered how long it had been since she'd allowed someone else to keep her safe. Then she remembered how strength could dominate and how that domination came larded with disrespect. She worked with men like that. She'd grown up with a man like that. She didn't need to sit in the lap of a man like that.

Bill stumbled to a halt.

Buffy spun around to watch and whacked Wyatt in the face with streamers of muddy hair. He spit mud out of his mouth. "You're as shaggy as your stupid buffalo." Something her father would have said.

Bill staggered, panting, still on his feet. Buffy held her breath. Bill sank to his front knees.

Shaw shoved his rifle back in its sling.

Shuddering with relief that Bill was sleeping and not dead, Buffy collapsed against Shaw's strong chest and let herself be held for a minute. "Thank you."

Shaw snorted.

Buffy remembered Bill might have a bullet in him. The

adrenaline was still roaring through her veins, and suddenly it exploded with nowhere to go. The whole mess caught up with her—being crushed under the gate panel, Sally's screams, the wild truck ride and the blazing gun, her near miss from Bill's horns, and this cowboy's grubby hands all over her.

She grabbed the front of Wyatt Shaw's black leather vest. She jerked him down. He didn't bend, so she ended up lifting herself until they were nose to nose. "Are you crazy? Shooting at my buffalo like that?" She shook him like she'd seen a cat shake a rat. He didn't budge, because he was twice her size and made, apparently, of forged steel, but she shook him anyway.

"Did you hit him?" she demanded. She let go of one side of his vest because she needed her hand. She jabbed him right in the second button of his blue chambray shirt. "If that buffalo dies because of you, I'm going to have the sheriff haul you in to—"

"Shut up," he spoke in a voice so grating it left rasp marks on her eardrums. The tone froze the words in her throat. "If I'd wanted him dead, he'd be dead. So—just—shut—up! Your animals are a menace."

Buffy leaned away from the rage.

Shaw leaned closer. "I've got a right to defend what's mine." His nose touched hers. "I rode over to meet the new boss and ended up saving your daughter's *life*."

He must mean Sally. Sally wasn't her daughter. She'd have pointed out yet another way he was wrong, but he wasn't done talking.

"I saved *your* life."

Her life? Huh! Bill had been seconds away from collapsing. She'd have been just fine. Of course, a couple of seconds with a buffalo stomping on you was a long time.

"But the thing that *matters* is—"

What did that mean: matters? Her life mattered—

"I saved my herd from having a bull buffalo running free in

it. If I hadn't been here to head him off, he could have spread disease to them. I could have lost a year's income while my cattle were quarantined. And that's not the only damage he could have done." Suddenly his face turned red, and his fiery hazel eyes blazed like wildfire. *"Your daughter isn't the only little kid out here!"*

She ducked quickly and began mentally swearing out the warrant for his arrest once she got a doctor to diagnose her whiplash. And then she'd sue him for every penny he had.

"I oughta sue you for every penny you have." With a swift, reckless motion, he lifted her off his saddle horn. He unceremoniously plunked her onto the ground. "If I ever catch one of your buffalo running wild again, I'll kill it, and then I'll be at your place with the sheriff." He wheeled his horse and took off at a gallop.

Buffy opened her mouth to yell all the things that had been boiling inside of her.

Wolf stepped between her and Shaw.

"What?" she snapped.

"I'm trying to turn your temper on me, which might save us from a million-dollar lawsuit."

Buffy looked for Shaw. He was just disappearing over a nearby rise. "Why shouldn't I yell at him?" She decided to take Wolf at his word and aim her temper at him. "You heard the things he said. You saw him shooting at Bill. That buff is worth a fortune. He's got the bloodlines the Commons needs. He's practically irreplaceable."

Wolf looked over his shoulder in the direction Shaw had gone. Good, he seemed to be finally figuring out what Shaw had almost done.

Wolf jabbed his thumb toward Shaw. "I reckon he thinks they're irreplaceable, too."

Two young children, accompanied by a woman, stepped up

so Buffy could see them against the expanse of South Dakota sky. They were right where Bill had headed when he'd taken off. Shaw had said Sally wasn't the only little kid in the world.

"They must have been out riding." Wolf crossed his arms as he studied the small group. "There's a wetland over there with a lake. The Shaws go picnicking right after church most Sundays. When Wyatt saw the buffalo tearing that way, he figured his twins were goners if he didn't do something drastic."

Buffy had to stop scowling and admit she was wrong, in every way, right down the line, which made her mad and set her to scowling again. She stared at Shaw, who pulled even with the children and swung himself off his horse with the graceful motion of a healthy animal. He turned back to look at her, and even from a distance that by now was a hundred yards, she could see him fuming. The woman took the horse's reins, and the boys grabbed his hands.

One of them hollered, "Did you shoot the buffaler, Dad?"

"Did you blow it into a million pieces of steak?" the other one asked.

The foursome dropped over the horizon.

"And he wasn't trying to kill the buffalo. He shot alongside it to turn it. He was herding it toward my tranq gun."

"That's why you told me not to drive straight toward Bill." Buffy glanced at Wolf. She'd only met him when she'd introduced herself as the new boss and arranged a crew to unload the bull she'd brought. But he had a reputation that was unrivaled when it came to buffalo. "You knew even then what he was doing?"

Wolf shrugged. His braids swung slightly against his beaded vest. "I thought maybe he had that in mind. It didn't matter if he was herding it toward us on purpose or by accident. Why get in his way?"

"He could have just missed," Buffy pointed out. "You said yourself it's nearly impossible to hit anything from the back of a running horse or the seat of a moving truck."

"That's me. That's most men. But Shaw, now there's a man who hits what he aims at. Oh, he was mad enough to kill the buff, and I thought at first he meant to. He'd've been within his rights."

Buffy heard an engine behind her and turned to see a rig, pulling the stock trailer they'd left behind, coming out to help. "The legal right to do something doesn't mean you should."

Wolf gave her a long considering look that set her back a little. His eyes were the bottomless black of his Sioux ancestors. His battered brown Stetson with the brightly beaded hatband was part of him, just like the buffalo and the land.

The solidness and wisdom of his gaze helped Buffy get ahold of herself. She had been overreacting from the minute that buffalo had slammed her into the ground. She could still feel the adrenaline humming.

"You aren't one'a them that puts an animal's life on an even keel with a human's, are you?" Wolf asked with cool interest. "I'm all for raisin' buff. I like the sight of them on this land, and it heals something in my soul to tend them. But if you think he should have let that buffalo hurt his children rather than shoot it, then I need to start job huntin'."

Buffy blanched. Wolf Running Shield had been here from the beginning. She had the credentials and the education to put a scientific face on this experiment in creating a buffalo commons in the Midwest, but she was just here for three months to work on her doctoral dissertation. Wolf was here for the duration. He was the man who ran this place. Without so much as an hour of college classes—and some suspicion about his years in high school—the man was a legend for his skill in handling buffalo. Leonard was calling Buffy the director of the Buffalo Commons because her advanced degrees put a shine on the place, but everyone knew Wolf was in charge.

If she had lost Bill, she'd have been fired. If she lost Wolf, they'd send her barefoot down a thorny road back to Oklahoma. They'd have her Doctor of Veterinary Medicine degree rescinded. They might assign her to study buffalo in another country, one where women had to wear veils. And she'd deserve it.

"I can't believe you said that." She sounded frantic, which she was. But she also meant it. Since she still had adrenaline coursing through her veins, she snapped, "Of course I don't think such a thing. I was just upset, and I didn't know his family was there. I'd have shot the bull myself before I let it touch one of those children."

"That's quite a hot button you got there, girl. You got any control over it?" Wolf asked, crossing his arms.

She took a couple of deep breaths and unclenched her fists. "I think having a buffalo run over me kind of overloaded my circuits. I'm sorry. And I shouldn't have yelled at Shaw either."

Buffy looked back at the now-empty horizon. "I suppose I owe the man an apology."

"And a thank-you," Wolf said.

She narrowed her eyes at the horizon. "I'd better hand that over, too."

"Yeah, Mr. Leonard is a stickler for community relations." Wolf mentioned the big boss, the one whose money was propping up this whole experiment.

"Besides that," Buffy muttered, "if I don't, I'm a coward and a lousy human being."

"Good point." Wolf walked away to kneel beside Bill and pull the dart out of his chest.

Buffy looked at the rolling hills of grass that looked level but hid swell after swell. It apparently also hid children and ponds, buffalo, and heavily armed ranchers.

The Commons truck pulled up. A cowhand climbed out. "We've never had one get away like that before. Wonder what riled him up?"

"He's a buffalo," Wolf said, as if that explained everything. Buffy decided it did.

Wolf nodded and turned to Buffy. "Might'ez well go on back to the house. We can handle this."

Buffy didn't like it. Wolf was testing her. Did she pass the test if she stayed to the bitter end? Or did she pass the test if she left the buffalo in his capable hands?

She didn't know—which was probably the real test.

Bill was as still as death. She went over and knelt beside him and laid her hands on his chest. It rose and fell steadily. He was strong, even lying here. He didn't need anybody. If someone pushed him, he pushed back hard. She fiercely loved him and his kind. She prayed every day she could be just like them.

She headed home to clean up and get on with her apology to Wyatt Shaw. But first she had a few things to say to Sally's irresponsible mother.

Jeanie had been through a terrible year since her tyrant of a husband had deserted her. Buffy was glad to see the end of Michael Davidson, but Jeanie had let the man run everything. Without him, she was lost, and she blamed herself for Michael's desertion. She covered her sense of failure with sullen indifference and occasional outright hostility.

Right now Buffy's temper was still simmering, and it might not be wise to confront Jeanie. If Jeanie got upset enough to leave, what would happen to Sally? Jeanie barely paid attention to the little sweetheart. But Buffy had to go in that house. And Jeanie wouldn't let Buffy get past her without saying something that Buffy would take exception to.

Feeling the full weight of messing up her first day at The Commons, dealing with her sister, and atoning for her rude behavior to Wyatt Shaw, Buffy trudged toward the house.

two

"I'm leaving." Jeanie swung the door open before Buffy got to it.

Having Jeanie on a rampage didn't alter Buffy's plans to keep cool.

Jeanie was three inches shorter, all blond curls bought at a beauty shop, generous curves, and pink lips used mainly for complaining.

Buffy was lanky, with straight brown hair that would have been in her standard no-nonsense braid if she hadn't lost her rubber band in the mud.

"You should have heard what that jerk said to me. I'm not living like this. Get us out of here."

"What did he say?"

"He glared at me and said, 'I got cows who're better baby-sitters than you.'"

Buffy choked on a laugh. "I'm sure he didn't mean it to sound as bad as it did. A mama cow is a very good mother. I'm going over to see him right now. I'll tell him how upset you were and insist he never speak to you again."

A calculating look came into Jeanie's eyes. "He was good-looking, wasn't he?"

"Who?" Buffy couldn't believe the turnaround. "Shaw? The jerk?"

Jeanie narrowed her eyes. "I didn't say I liked him. I just noticed he was attractive."

Jeanie had to find a new man to run her life one of these days. Shaw might be the perfect answer, but Buffy couldn't quite squash her uneasiness. "I'm on my way over to see the good-looking jerk. He helped me catch Bill."

"Who is Bill?" Jeanie brushed her mauve fingertips through her blond hair.

"Bill?" Buffy prompted. "The buffalo we just spent two days hauling across three states?"

"Oh yeah, him." Jeanie waved away the buffalo that was so dear to Buffy's heart.

"Anyway, Mr. Leonard is big on community relations. So now I need to face a very angry man and apologize. I expect him to hand me my head. If you want to ask him out on a date, I'll take my head and quietly hold it in my lap while you hit on him."

Jeanie sniffed. "I'll wait until he's not quite so mad. You go fix the mess you made, and maybe I'll drive over and see him in a week or so."

"Okay." Buffy nodded her head, and a clump of muddy hair came unglued from the rat's nest on her head and swung around and slapped her in the face. "I'm going to take a shower first."

Jeanie sniffed again, and this time Buffy was pretty sure that it was a commentary on how Buffy smelled.

Jeanie had cut ties with their parents when, over their father's objections, she ran off to marry Michael. Buffy had cut those same ties just because she had a functioning brain.

Now Jeanie had nowhere to go and no one to do her thinking for her except Buffy—not a job Buffy had applied for. She walked away before she could say any of the things she wanted to—about how hard work sometimes got a person dirty, and it was nothing to sniff at, and Jeanie should try it sometime.

☙

"An' then you pulled your gun and blasted that nasty ol' buffaler right into a million pieces of steak, right, Dad?" Cody acted out the gunshot and fell to the ground in a poor imitation of a dying buffalo.

"You took out your gun, and you hung from the neck of your horse, holding the reins in your teeth." Colt snagged the collar of his T-shirt between his teeth and talked around the fabric. "Then you blew him away."

Cody started shooting his finger at Colt. Colt "died" with a lot of screaming; then he sprang to his feet and started shooting back. The boys ran in circles, shrieking and pretending games of horrible, painful death—all in good fun.

The house wasn't large. The upstairs family room had been converted to a makeshift bedroom for Wyatt's sixteen-year-old niece, Anna, for the summer. Anna had come faithfully every summer since Jessica had died. Wyatt didn't know what he'd have done without her for the last four years.

Wyatt turned the page on the Sunday paper and let the boys scream and knock over the kitchen furniture.

It kept them occupied.

He was sitting there when he heard a pounding on his front door. Once he noticed it, he had the impression that maybe the pounding had been going on for a while. He'd just chalked the sound up to thundering footsteps and falling bodies. He laid aside his paper irritably. "Who in Sam Hill comes to my front door?"

Wyatt had to go into a room he never used, although Anna had dusted it the other day. He went to the front door and had to fiddle with the dead bolt for a while, because he didn't remember which way to turn it. "I'm coming. Hold your"—he swung open the door on that little wildcat from the Buffalo Commons—"horses."

"What about horses?" she asked.

Something short-circuited in his brain. She looked a lot different when she wasn't covered with mud. A lot better. She was wearing a blue jean skirt that hung nearly to her ankles and a loose-fitting white blouse.

She had brown eyes, light like warm baked earth, and one smooth, fat braid draped over her shoulder that hung nearly to her waist. Without the mud and the bad temper and the mind made up to hate him, she was about the prettiest thing he'd ever seen.

He just stood there and stared.

And she stared right back.

Finally the gracious host in him kicked in. "What're you doin' here?"

Her eyes hardened.

What kind of nonsense was going on in her head now? He waited.

She glared.

His boys saved him. They crashed into him so hard he staggered forward, almost into her.

He caught himself; then he caught the two boys, one in each hand.

She looked away from him, examined each of the twins for a second, and smiled.

Rats, it was a great smile. And he'd gotten close enough to find out she smelled great, too.

She bent down toward his boys. "Hi, did you guys see that buffalo this afternoon?"

Wyatt looked down at the twins. Their eyes got so wide and serious they could have been watching Jesus come again and realized they'd yet to repent. After a stunned silence—a small miracle in itself—they started yelling.

Cody went first. "Dad left us to play by the lake while he went over to meet the new boss at the buffalo ranch."

"We saw the buffaler charge right over the hill." Colt bounced.

"We were running for the tree, but it's too high to climb." Cody waved his arms as if he'd considered flying to safety.

Colt added, "We were trying to save Anna when Dad came charging on Gumby."

She glanced at Wyatt. "Gumby?"

"Then he pulled his rifle and blew it away." Cody acted that out with sound effects and flailing arms.

"The boys named him," Wyatt said.

The buffalo gal said to Cody, "He didn't blow it away."

Cody nodded frantically. "Into a billion pieces of buffalo steak."

Wyatt noticed that Cody's steaks kept getting more plentiful. That could mean he was hungry.

"What are your names?"

Wyatt wondered if that was a sly jab at his lack of manners. Or maybe she just wanted to know their names.

"I'm Cody."

She stared at him with fixed attention for slightly too long, and Wyatt wondered what she was thinking.

"I'm Colt."

She gave Colt the same close examination.

Colt went into his favorite part of the made-up story. "He hung on to the reins with his teeth."

Dividing her attention between the boys, she said, "I'm glad you're all right. Your father saved you and Anna. He saved me." She laid her hand on her throat and crouched down so she was eye level with the boys.

The boys moved past him so they were between Wyatt and the woman, which struck Wyatt as a good idea. He didn't like her being so close.

She rested a hand on each of the boys' shoulders. "And he saved my niece, Sally, a tiny little three-year-old girl who was right in the way of terrible danger. Your father is a hero over and over."

Both boys were struck dumb. Another moment of silence—unheard of. They stared at her for a frozen minute then launched themselves at her, and each grabbed a hand. They started tugging her inside, and Wyatt had to step back or be run over. Or worse yet, smell her again.

She gave him a startled look.

He shrugged and stepped farther out of the way. "Come on in, I guess."

As they dragged her past him, she said, "I'm Allison Lange."

"Wyatt Shaw."

"Call me Buffy."

The boys quit manhandling her and stared in awe.

"Buffy, like in *buffalo*?" Colt spoke first, which was unusual. Cody usually talked for the pair, but he looked stunned.

Cody found his voice. "You're named after the buffalo?"

"I love buffalo, and I've spent my whole life studying them. The nickname sort of sneaked up on me."

Wyatt snorted. "Your whole life? What are you, twenty?"

Allison said severely, "Twenty-five."

"Well, 'scuse me."

"How old are you, fifty?" She narrowed her eyes.

The boys couldn't stop staring. Wyatt was having a little trouble himself. "No, I'm twenty-five."

She glanced at his six-year-olds and raised an eyebrow at him.

"I started young."

"I'll say."

The boys fell on her again and dragged her fully into Jessica's formal living room. Jessica had wanted a room just for entertaining guests. Trouble was they never had any guests except the ones who came in the kitchen door and plunked themselves down at the kitchen table. They more often than not had muddy boots on and wanted to talk about baling hay or castrating bull calves. So Jessica hadn't wanted them in her nice room anyway. Wyatt would have done anything to ease Jessica's unhappiness, and he was glad to let her do up this room all formal; in the end, it just reminded her of how disappointed she was with her life. Now this room existed as a kind of shrine to her memory and a sharp poke in the eye to Wyatt if he ever got lonely for a woman.

"How did you get named after a buffaler?"

"Was it one buffalo? A special one?"

"Dad had the teeth in his reins. . .I mean, the reins in his teeth."

"Colt, I never had the reins in my teeth."

"Do you want me to bring coffee for the lady?" Anna came into the room, her eyes lively with curiosity. Anna, dark haired like Wyatt and his boys, was as tall as a woman but still had the gangly figure of a teen. But she was mature and as smart as a whip. She had to be to stay ahead of Wyatt's boys.

Cody jerked his thumb at Allison-Buffy Lange. "Her name is Buffalo."

Colt chimed in. "She said Dad is a hero. He saved the whole town from a rampaging buffalo."

Cody shoved his brother and ran toward Anna, still dragging Allison. "Mrs. Buffalo fights buffalo just like dad. She shoots them and blows them into a zillion pieces of steak."

"Are you hungry, Cody?" Wyatt asked. That was a question that, in his son's whole life, only had one answer.

Both boys began shouting about how hungry they were.

"I want steak. Can we have buffalo steak?" Cody—of course.

"No! Cookies!" Colt shoved Cody sideways. "Anna made chocolate chip cookies yesterday."

"We ate them all, stupid," Cody sneered.

"I'm not stupid. You're stupid." Colt launched himself at Cody.

"I hid some," Anna announced. The teenager was wise beyond her years. "This way." She pointed at the kitchen.

Both boys quit wrestling, yelled, and headed out of the room, abandoning Allison and dragging Anna with them, telling her all about what Mrs. Buffalo had said, or rather their wildly altered version of it.

"Dad's a hero. He saved a hundred lives," Cody said.

Colt shouted, "That's more'n Spiderman."

"That's more'n Spiderman and Superman combined." Cody elbowed Colt and ran.

Anna glanced over her shoulder. "I'll bring coffee in a minute." She followed the boys into the kitchen.

His guest sank into a chair and stared after the boys.

Wyatt tried his best not to smile. Then he remembered who he was dealing with, and it was easy not to smile.

She turned to him. "Where do they get all that energy?"

"They tap it straight out of my bloodstream. I'm half dead by nightfall." He said it lightly, but it irritated him that she seemed so horrified by his children.

"My niece is a handful, but she can't touch the two of them."

He hung on to his patience. "Your niece?"

Allison nodded. "Yes, Sally, the little girl whose life you saved this afternoon, right before you saved your three children."

Wyatt's temper cooled a little. "Anna's my niece. She's staying for the summer to babysit."

"That's good. 'Cuz she'd've been born when you were about nine."

"She *was* born when I was nine. But my sister and her husband were doing the honors, so no one considered me too young." He was flirting. He ran into a mental brick wall as the idea bloomed to life in his head. He hadn't flirted with a woman since he'd fallen in love with Jessica in college.

Allison returned to buffalo talk. "You didn't just save Sally and your family. You herded my buffalo toward me so we could tranquilize him. Then you saved me."

"After Wolf had already done it once. Not to mention being nearly crushed under that gate when you let that beast get loose to begin with." Wyatt changed his tone, determined to push Allison out of his head and out of his house. "And I understand you're the new boss? Great."

"Only for a while. The permanent boss comes in a few months. I have the credentials Mr. Leonard wants for his buffalo ranch, but Wolf will still run the day-to-day operations."

"You've spent most of this day screwing up big-time, Allison."

Allison didn't react as he expected. "And it's early. I'll be half dead by nightfall. And call me Buffy. It's gotten so I can't remember being Allison."

"Well, Sunday is my day of rest, so from now on, you're on your own. . .um, Buffy." He shook his head. "I can't call you that. You look nothing like a buffalo."

She smiled. "Thanks. So there you were, saving people right and left. And by way of thanks, I shouted at you."

Wyatt felt compelled to add, "And strangled me, and poked me in the chest, and called me crazy, and threatened to set the sheriff on me, and—"

Buffy held up her hand. "Enough, please. I'll be here all day apologizing. Surely you want to get rid of me."

Wyatt thought how true that was, and he was poised to say so when Anna came back in with the coffee. "The boys said Uncle Wyatt saved your life. We were down by the lake when all this happened. We just barely caught a glimpse of the buffalo before Uncle Wyatt drove it away. Tell me about it."

So Buffy, instead of being politely but rapidly dismissed as Wyatt had planned, settled in to tell the whole story, complete with Sally screaming and her own near death under a gate. Then the grand finale, when she was snatched from the jaws of death—or the horns of death—by Wyatt's heroic action.

Wyatt gritted his teeth when his boys came in and listened with silent fascination to the whole tale, which Buffy recounted far more dramatically than Wyatt thought was necessary, casting him in a superhero role that easily outdid Spiderman and Superman on their best days. That's all he needed—more stimulation for the boys.

Buffy talked with her hands and did Wyatt's voice, almost echoing with valor, and Wolf's voice, wise and deep. She did herself, weak and terrified, in the very best tradition of a damsel in distress. It was alive and dramatic. Wyatt thought, with a little work, she could make it on Broadway. She glowed while she talked, every emotion vivid and full. He couldn't take his eyes off her.

When she was done, the boys began to act it out, with a lot more screaming than Buffy had included and way more shooting.

It broke the spell she'd put him under. Wyatt stood the racket and Buffy's pretty face as long as he could, and finally, when the boys had dashed outside so they could create their drama on a larger stage, he said, "Well, I need to get back to my day of rest."

He watched her looking nervously after his boys, and when she didn't take his hint, he stood, took her hand, and towed her gently but firmly out of Jessica's fussy chair. Touching her was a mistake. Her hand was callused from hard work, but the back of it was as smooth as silk. She was tanned almost as dark as he was. Everything about her said she was an outdoor girl who loved animals and the country, everything his wife hadn't been. He had to get her out of here.

He escorted her firmly toward the door and booted a rather surprised Mrs. Buffalo out of his house and left her standing on his front porch. He only let her out that way because he wanted her to be able to find her truck.

He was going to close the door in her face and hope that eventually she'd figure it out and go home. Then, because she had that strange look in her eyes like his boys had frightened her more than that charging buffalo this afternoon, a perverse streak kicked in. "You know, talk is cheap, Buffalo Gal. If you're not up to controlling that menace you call a buffalo commons, then get out and take your buffalo with you."

Her eyes focused a little, and he thought he saw something worse than a woman who didn't like his children. He saw a woman who didn't like herself very much.

That strange flash of self-doubt faded from her eyes quickly, and she replaced it with her sharp tongue. "What's your real problem with me and my buffalo? Today was bad, and I can't thank you enough for your help, but you were already angry with the Commons before Bill got away."

"My problem is, your boss is an arrogant city boy whose money is screwing up this whole country. His dream is to own every acre of land out here and let buffalo roam loose on it."

"He buys it. He doesn't steal it from anyone. Who cares what he does with it?"

"I care. He pays too much for it. He's so rich he doesn't need to make the land pay, so every time a piece of land comes up for sale, he outbids every rancher in the area, which locks out any chance for young men to get a start or for established ranchers to expand their holdings."

"Meaning you," she accused flatly.

"Yes, meaning me. I have wanted to add to my land for a long time, but I've butted up against Leonard everywhere. He practically owns all of the land in a circle around the S Bar."

"If he's willing to pay it, then that's what it's worth. That's how supply and demand works. Maybe you've heard of it? Capitalism?"

"And my taxes skyrocket because he's pushed land values up. This land doesn't return much per acre, because the watering holes are far apart, wells are expensive to dig and maintain, and the grasslands are broken up by the rugged foothills. But your boss comes in here and doesn't need it to pay 'cuz he's rich. It's the same as if someone came waltzing in here and offered to do your job for free. It doesn't hurt them because they're rich, but maybe, just maybe, you need that pesky money to feed yourself."

Indignantly, Buffy swung her braid over her shoulder. Wyatt followed the graceful movement of her head and tried to remember why he was yelling at her. She jammed her fists against her waist and reminded him. "This area once belonged to the buffalo. They are native to it, and it's more natural to have them roaming than your cattle. You're the newcomer here, not my buffalo."

"Newcomer? My great-great-grandfather homesteaded this land. Shaws have lived here since before South Dakota became a state. If I'm a newcomer, what are you?"

"I'm tending what is natural. If I had my way, this whole state and North Dakota, Nebraska, Kansas, Oklahoma, Northern Texas, Wyoming, and Colorado, all the way to the Rockies, would be part of the Buffalo Commons. You just said yourself this land barely supports a cattle herd. Mr. Leonard can't do it all himself, but eventually, with the help of a lot of well-intentioned people, we're giving this land back to nature the way God intended."

Wyatt knew this was at the heart of Leonard's Buffalo Commons. He'd always known, although no one ever admitted it out loud. He had a feeling Buffy wouldn't be doing it right now if she wasn't so upset. "Giving it back to God? You just displaced about twenty million people and wiped out eighty percent of America's beef supply. Where are we all supposed to live? What are we supposed to eat?"

"I'm a vegetarian, so I'll be fine, and as for where you live—"

She poked him in the chest, which took them right back to where they'd been this afternoon. Wyatt decided right then he wasn't going to be nearly as polite about her next apology—

"I hear there's a lot of empty space in Siberia these days. How about that?"

"A vegetarian?" Wyatt snorted. "I suppose you're one of those PETA freaks who are always vandalizing medical labs and posing naked on billboards protesting fur."

"I've got my membership card in the car. National, state, and local chapters."

Wyatt grabbed her hand to make her stop digging a hole in his chest and leaned down until he was right in her face. "There aren't any local chapters. This is South Dakota. We have a hunting season on people who won't eat meat."

And right when he was going to really let her have it, give her the full and final send-off—which he hadn't thought of yet but figured he'd just yell until it came to him—the boys charged around the corner of the house, shooting each other, of course.

She said tartly, "Maybe instead of a *hunting* season, you ought to try an *education* season to teach children shooting isn't a game."

Wyatt almost choked. His rage faded into something hard and cold and bitter. He'd been furious with her, but he'd had political debates with people and never went away mad.

Through clenched teeth he said, "I don't have to stand here and listen to an educated idiot insult my children. You may have college degrees coming out of your ears, but anyone who lets a buffalo loose in a yard full of people is either incompetent or stupid. I'm betting you're both."

He glared at her and saw her eyes widen. She lifted her hand to cover her mouth, glanced at his boys, and said from behind her fingers, "I'm sorry. I didn't mean to insult your boys. They're wonderful. I was upset, and I shouldn't have—"

His boys charged up to her. They looked at her with shining

eyes and included her in their hero worship.

Wyatt wondered how much they'd heard.

"There's cookies left. And we're having buffaler steak for supper. Why don't you stay?" Colt grabbed her hand.

She bent over him and ran her free hand over his dark hair. "I'm sorry, Colt. I have to get back to my own place."

"How do you know it's me?" Colt's heart was in his eyes.

She said kindly, "Why, you're Colt." She looked sideways at Cody and brushed her hand in an identical motion over Cody's unruly curls. "And you're Cody."

"But no one can tell us apart. 'Cept Dad," Cody said in awe. "We even fool Anna all the time."

Wyatt saw both of them fall completely in love with her in that instant, and he wanted to scream at her for making them care when she held them and him and their whole life in contempt.

She glanced up at him and visibly flinched at what she saw in his eyes. *Good.*

"I'm sorry."

"You're sorry you can tell us apart?" Cody said, confused. "Is that what an *educated idiot* means?"

So they'd heard that. Had they heard her make that crack about them shooting at each other? Of course, truth be told, Wyatt got a little tired of the constant shooting, too.

"No, I'm not sorry I can tell you apart," she said awkwardly. "I was telling your dad I was sorry."

"For what? What'd ya do? We have to say we're sorry all the time." Colt added in a deadly serious voice, "And we have to mean it."

She looked so sorry and was being so nice to the boys, but Wyatt had been married to Jessica too long to ignore the words that came out in the heat of the moment. In his experience, that was the only time a woman told the truth.

"Tell us again about what a hero Dad was," Cody demanded. "We want to hear the part where the buffalo stabbed you with his horns and was shaking you to death when Dad yanked you loose."

"I want to hear the part when Dad jumped on the buffalo's back with a knife in his teeth." Colt started chewing on his shirt collar again.

"Miss Lange has to go now, boys. You've already heard the story. Say good-bye."

She laid her hand on his arm. "Don't do this. Don't send me away without accepting my apology. You've got to forget I said that. I'm around buffalo too much. I've forgotten how to watch my mouth."

"Or you've forgotten how to lie." Wyatt grabbed both boys by the hands and pulled them, protesting at the top of their lungs, into the house.

They took off toward the kitchen, shooting at each other again.

"Wyatt, please. Wait."

He slammed the door in her face; then he clicked the lock on the front door so hard he felt it snap inside the door. He fumbled with it a second and realized he'd broken it. The door was locked for good. Wyatt looked around the room. His shrine. His reminder. Suddenly he knew he didn't need Jessica to remind him of how a woman could be. He had a new neighbor who'd be doing that better than Jessica ever had.

"Boys, how'd you like a bigger bedroom?" he yelled loud enough to draw them back from their wild-game hunt. . .or wild-cookie hunt probably.

They returned, still protesting the loss of Mrs. Buffalo, but the offer of more space turned their attention.

"Sure, Dad," Cody said.

How had she been able to tell the boys apart? They were so

identical that Jessica had left their hospital bracelets on until they were nearly two, taking them in to have them replaced when they got tight. Little more than toddlers, they'd already learned to trick her all the time, right up until she died four years ago. They'd made a joke out of it, but he knew it had hurt them that their own mother couldn't tell them apart.

"Are you going to build on to the house?" Colt tugged on the leg of Wyatt's blue jeans.

"No, we're going to throw out this old pink furniture and move you in here." Wyatt swept his arm to erase all of Jessica's fussy, perfect details.

Colt and Cody exploded into hyperactive joy.

Anna came in to see what the trouble was. She got excited when Wyatt told her he was making the boys' bedroom into a room for her. "What brought this on?" she asked.

"I'd just about forgotten this room existed is all. I can't believe I've let this space go to waste."

"When do we start?"

"Right now," Wyatt said through clenched teeth.

Anna gave him a worried look.

"I'm going to hitch up the stock trailer and start hauling things outside." He glanced at the broken door and was suddenly furious that he couldn't open it. He'd have to take it off its hinges. He blamed that inconvenience on Mrs. Buffalo, too.

He heard a truck start up and drive slowly out of the driveway. Only now did Wyatt realize that Buffy must have stood in the yard all this time, probably hating herself for insulting his children, the one thing any parent—which she wasn't—would know was unforgivable.

A little voice in Wyatt's head whispered, "Nothing is unforgivable."

Wyatt looked over at the picture Jessica had hung over the back of the couch. It was a radiant sunset. The stark silhouette of an empty cross stood black against the glorious sky. Across the bottom of the picture blazed the words, JESUS IS THE LIGHT OF THE WORLD.

On this he and Jessica had agreed. They'd been at odds on so much, but they'd tried to accept their differences, sometimes with grim patience, and respect the commitment they'd made before God. This picture was the one thing he wasn't going to throw away.

He tried to harden his heart. He tried to ignore the picture. But he was wrong. Buffy had apologized, and she'd meant it. She'd been arguing with him mainly because he'd been hassling her from the moment she'd come here with her gracious apology and her exaggerated story of his own heroism—a gift to his children that they would cherish all their lives. Or at least until they were teenagers and figured out what a weirdo their dad was.

Yes, she'd said something rude when he'd pushed her to the brink. But she'd immediately regretted it. He'd seen that clearly in her eyes.

He listened to the fading sound of her truck and knew the truth, disgusting as it was. He needed to forgive her. Even more that that, he owed her an apology.

He stared sightlessly through the walls of his house across the miles to the Buffalo Commons. He had to go over there. It was his turn to grovel. At this rate, they'd wear out their tires slinking back and forth with their grudging apologies. Except hers hadn't been grudging; hers had been beautiful. She was beautiful.

He shook his head to clear it of the way she looked and smiled and smelled. He'd do it, and he'd get out before either of them could make it worse. And then that would be the end. He'd make it a point to never see that snippy little city girl again.

He said to his rioting boys, "I'll call the secondhand store in town in the morning and make sure they'll take the stuff. We can load the stock trailer now then move your stuff in. No reason you can't sleep in here tonight."

"Uncle Wyatt?" Anna said doubtfully.

"Huh?"

"Uh, the room is kind of. . .pink for the boys."

The boys froze as they studied the pink walls. They looked at their father in horror.

Pink! What had his wife been thinking? There were frills and flowers everywhere. She'd created a room so out of place on a ranch that no one could be comfortable in it.

Wyatt looked at his sons' faces, alive with dread that they'd have to choose between a new room with pink walls or no new room at all. For a man who was feeling sick from having to slither on his belly to tell a woman he was sorry for being a jerk, he almost smiled. It was just as well he did feel like smiling. He didn't think he'd be doing much smiling once the Buffalo Gal had her say.

"Okay. We paint as soon as the furniture goes. If the store can take this old stuff tomorrow morning, I'll run it into town and buy paint. We'll paint tomorrow afternoon, and you move in here Tuesday."

The boys resumed their joyful ruckus, and Wyatt thought grumpily of the helping of crow he was going to have to swallow.

three

"Somebody ought to lock me up." Buffy sat in the front seat of her truck, resting her forehead against the steering wheel.

"I can't believe I said that. God, why did I say that?" She'd been praying the same prayer nonstop since Wyatt Shaw had slammed his door in her face. She wasn't any closer to an answer beyond she was stupid and rude.

She'd always believed that when someone did something truly awful to her, she could chalk it up to "stupid or rude." It was a simple test that satisfied a person's hurt feelings because either answer left one feeling superior. Now she had to use the test on herself.

"Am I stupid or rude?"

God was silent.

She heard a snuffling sound and looked over at Bill nosing his little corral. Bill's nose poked through the massive timbers that stretched for miles across the prairie, penning in over a thousand head of buffalo in a 54,000-acre pasture that wound along the edges of the Black Hills National Park. She tried to absorb Bill's strength and let it soothe her soul.

Instead, she remembered telling Wyatt to move to Siberia. She had told him she wanted all the other people in South Dakota and the rest of the Midwest to go away, too. She'd driven past Omaha on her way out here. A million people living in the metro area according to the road map. Where in Siberia were they supposed to go? Instead of fencing buffalo in, she'd have to slap up a fence around a million people so a herd of buffalo wouldn't come stampeding down the interstate during rush hour.

When she'd heard about the Buffalo Commons, she'd looked at the map and the vast open spaces, and she hadn't really thought about these few little towns in the Midwest. Now she'd figured out there were ten thousand little towns, and where were the people living in them supposed to go? Somewhere. They'd move. Big deal.

She banged her head on the steering wheel. "Stupid? Rude? Stupid? Rude? Easy." She looked up at the roof of her truck. "You don't need to bother answering, God. It's easy. I'm both."

She tried to remember what else she'd said. She was sure she hadn't plumbed the depths of this afternoon's stupidity and rudeness. Of course, first, last, and always, she'd insulted his boys. He'd taken everything else pretty well. He'd seemed to hate her no matter what she said or did, but besides that, he'd taken it well. And then she'd taken a shot at his children. She banged her head on the steering wheel for a while longer.

"Aunt Buffy?"

Buffy turned her head and looked through her open window. Sally, outside alone again. She hesitated, thinking maybe she was too stupid and rude to be this close to little children. In the end, she risked Sally's welfare and opened the door, because she needed a hug.

So that made her stupid, rude, *and* selfish. Buffy moaned.

"Are you all right?" Sally said with a little furrow between her brows.

"C'mere, honey." Buffy reached out her arms, and Sally scrambled up onto the seat. Buffy scooted over so Sally wasn't squished between her and the steering wheel.

"What'za matter, Aunt Buffy?" Sally laid her chubby hands on Buffy's face and held her head so she couldn't look away.

Buffy smiled at the little sweetheart. She was a mirror image of Jeanie, with her white blond ringlets and perfect pink cheeks and blue eyes that showed everything she felt.

"I'm feeling bad about letting that buffalo get away today." Suddenly Buffy remembered Sally's screams. Her heart lurched, and she clutched Sally tight to her. The image of Sally, crushed and dead under Bill's heels, was almost too much to bear. "I'm so glad you weren't hurt, honey. So glad."

She gave Sally a kiss on the top of her head and made her decision between stupid and rude. She knew exactly how bad it could have been. And she knew what she'd do to prevent it from happening again. She was *not* stupid.

That left rude. She decided that was better. A person could learn some manners, but stupid was forever.

With a hefty sigh, she knew she needed to go apologize yet again. But not tonight. She was too tired and frazzled. She'd probably just end up being rude again and digging herself in deeper. Besides, Wyatt might shoot her on sight.

Sally said, "Can we go inside, Aunt Buffy? I'm hungry."

Buffy looked at the darkened sky. It was midsummer, and the days were long. It had to be after nine o'clock. How long had she sat there talking at the Shaws'? She'd actually been having fun for a while. Then she'd come home, changed into work clothes, and done chores alongside her hired men, her conscience poking at her for being away from the job.

Because she didn't want to go in and listen to Jeanie whine anymore, she'd climbed back in her truck and sat, feeling sorry for herself. "Didn't you get any supper?"

"Nope, Mommy was tired after the long drive. She said for me to find something in the refrigerator, but there's nothing there."

Buffy slid out of the pickup with Sally still in her arms. She began walking toward the house. "Of course there's nothing there. We just moved in today. But we'll figure something out, or else we'll run out and get burgers."

"Is there a McDonald's around here?"

Buffy stopped short. She looked in all directions. She knew the main road led to a town, but it was tiny. No doubt the sidewalks rolled up at nine o'clock—if they had sidewalks. She shook her head and started for the house again. "We'll just find something here. We don't want to drive a long way this late at night anyway."

"Okay," Sally said with perfect trust.

Buffy carried her into the house, so tired and demoralized she was having trouble lifting her feet.

Supper ended up being a can of tomato soup—the only thing Buffy could rustle up from the bare pantry shelves. She started a grocery list and helped Sally with a bath. Then she found the room Sally was to sleep in with boxes piled everywhere and no sheets on the bed. She'd asked Jeanie to take care of this.

Afraid of what she'd say if she found Jeanie, she made the bed herself, digging for Sally's pajamas and ferreting out a set of sheets and a blanket. Sally was falling asleep before Buffy finished. Digging out the baby monitor, Buffy took it to her room, not surprised to find out she had to make her own bed. She took another quick shower to rinse the sweat off her body so she could sleep. She was near collapse when she lay down.

She assumed Jeanie had gone to bed without a thought to Sally's supper or sleeping arrangements, let alone Buffy's. She also knew it wasn't safe to assume anything with Jeanie, but she didn't check on her sister. As she adjusted the volume on the monitor, it hit her anew as she lay there that she'd insulted Wyatt's children. She covered her face with both hands and wondered if the moan was the Holy Spirit praying for her.

There was a Bible verse that said, "We do not know what we ought to pray for, but the Spirit himself intercedes for us with groans that words cannot express." She hoped the Spirit was praying for her now, because Buffy couldn't put it all into words, all that she'd done wrong today.

"Maybe I am stupid after all," she suggested to God.

She got an idea then. It wasn't a still, small voice or a bolt of lightning, but she thought it came from God all the same because it was 180 degrees from the direction of her thoughts. It was simple.

She was forgiven.

She'd start over tomorrow. She'd apologize to everyone, maybe even Jeanie for being forced to live a hundred feet from the end of the earth because of a buffalo obsession.

"God, what other choice do I have anyway?"

The turmoil in her soul settled, and she slept.

❧

Wyatt felt differently about apologizing to Buffy by the time he'd tossed and turned all night, rehearsing.

She hated him.

He hated her.

It was a system he could live with.

Then Cody kicked Anna in the shin and told her she was an educated idiot. The fistfight that followed between his boys was their usual exaggerated reenactment of everything their father said and did, which meant he'd better start setting a good example.

Wyatt took the boys with him to buy paint and pitched in on the painting until noon.

While they ate, Wyatt said, "I've got to quit helping with the room for a while, guys. I've got to go over and apologize to the Buffalo Gal. I was rude to her yesterday, and when a man is rude, he's got to say he's sorry."

Cody and Colt looked at him, blinking.

Wyatt doubted they got the lesson.

Then they went nuts, begging to come, and started tearing around the room hunting imaginary buffalo.

"We want to see Mrs. Buffalo again," Cody kept shouting.

Colt rushed up to him and grabbed his hand then went back to attacking Cody.

Wyatt didn't want them along. They would open themselves up to more insults, and they'd fall further in love with that East-Coast-liberal, PETA-freak, buffalo-loving neighbor of theirs, who would no doubt dress up like a carrot and picket his ranch on her days off.

"Please take them, Uncle Wyatt. They're driving me nuts with all their help," Anna added good-naturedly, holding up a paintbrush in the room, now so empty it echoed. "You two have got to quit shooting at each other all the time."

Wyatt didn't feel so much as a twinge of anger at Anna for the exactly same insult that he had refused to forgive Buffy for, so he was all the more aware of his need to grovel.

A cowardly streak Wyatt wasn't proud of prompted him to let the boys come. Buffy might not leave as deep of bite marks when she bit his head off if the boys were witnesses.

He loaded them in the truck, having to wage a war to keep them out of the back end and another one to get them in their seat belts. Then he took off to crawl on his belly.

❧

"Buffy, Bill came up lame this morning. You'd better have a look at that cut on his leg."

Wolf and three hired men were crowding Bill with a heavy panel until he stepped through the head gate, which snapped on his neck. There was a bucket of corn under his nose, and although some buffalo fought the gate until they were a danger to themselves, Bill just started munching.

Buffy climbed in with her vet bag and found a deep gouge on his hind leg. Bill did his best to kick her head off while she and Wolf tied the leg so she could stitch it. She gave Bill a shot of antibiotics and measured his height and weight on the underground scale he stood on, all data she needed for her doctoral research.

"Bill survived both the trip and his wild run across the prairie with no serious injuries and no weight loss." She flinched when Bill's leg slipped loose and whipped past Wolf's head, even though the buffalo never quit gobbling the corn.

"And no loss of his bad attitude." Wolf centered his hat back on his head.

Buffy peered around Bill's side, smiled, and checked her clipboard to compare Bill's vital statistics against the data she'd been given at the animal preserve in Oklahoma.

By the time she was done, she was soaked with sweat, Bill had slammed her into the fence a dozen times, and she'd eaten half her weight in dirt.

She moved away, and Wolf released Bill from the gate. Once he was free, Bill just stayed in the same spot eating until the corn was gone.

Wolf laughed as they climbed the fence. "Bill spent the last half hour trying to kill us, and now he's loose, and he doesn't even bother to run away."

Buffy looked down at her filthy clothes and sure-to-be-bruised arms; then she smiled fondly at the stubborn bull. "I suppose it makes me weird, but I love buffalo and I love this life."

"Me, too." Wolf leaned against the fence. Buffy stood beside Wolf and looked through the heavy wooden fence, listening to the quiet crunch of Bill cropping grass. Then Wolf got back to work. "We've already separated out the other old bull so it's safe to turn Bill into the herd. Bill has the makings of an alpha male, but he might need a couple of years to grow into it. The old bull will sense that."

"Yeah, they'd fight, and there's no reason to risk one of them getting hurt." Buffy made a few more notations on her clipboard; then she looked up at Wolf and smiled. "We'll ship the old bull down to Mr. Leonard's Oklahoma ranch and let him run with that herd for the next couple of years. It reduces the risk of narrowing the gene pool."

Wolf shrugged, and his leathered face almost curved into a smile. "I don't know about genetics, but I know it's not a good idea to let a herd get inbred."

Buffy handed the clipboard to Wolf, jerked her leather gloves off, and tucked them behind her belt buckle. She wiped the sleeve of her blue chambray shirt across her dripping forehead. "We're just putting scientific lingo to something any good rancher has known for centuries."

Wolf nodded at the herd of buffalo milling across the fence from Bill.

Resting her arms on the rugged boards, Buffy felt a slight breeze ruffling in the July heat cool the back of her sweat-soaked shirt. She and Wolf shared a moment of harmony as they watched the big animals.

"Listen, Wolf, I want you to know I respect what you're doing here. They call me the boss, but it's only on paper because Mr. Leonard likes college degrees on his staff. Even the guy who's coming to replace me doesn't have your experience. You run this place. You should have the house."

"I don't need it and you do. I'm happy in that fancy trailer Mr. Leonard pulled in."

"So I was told. But, well, we both know who's in charge. Don't doubt it. I know where I went wrong yesterday, not wiring those gates and working where the footing was wet, but I want you to tell me how you've done all of this before. I don't plan to change anything. The reports I've gotten on the Commons are too good. I want to document it. It's all going into my doctoral dissertation. I'm doing a case study of how to reintroduce buffalo to the wild."

"I'm not going to be a good sport about it if I hit one with my truck."

Buffy spun around at the intrusive voice.

Of course it was Shaw, come to hand her her head, no doubt.

She squared her shoulders, determined to take whatever he dished out and not say a word. Cody and Colt hit her with hurricane force, and she staggered back against the fence. She felt the hot puff of Bill's breath on her neck.

"Hi, Mrs. Buffalo."

"Hi, Colt." She smiled at his impish face. Cody tried to get out of her arms and run toward Bill. She sighed.

"You knew me again!" Colt shouted just inches from her face.

Bill snorted at the commotion.

"Cody, you stay away from that fence!" Buffy said. "Can't you look at Bill and know he's nobody you should be messing with?"

"Bill? This is Bill? The buffalo Dad chased across the open prairie while he tried to kill a hundred people?"

Buffy glanced at Wyatt.

He shrugged. "You're the one who made it into a stage production."

She had to admit that was right. "Yes, this is Bill."

"He's in the pen. He can't hurt me," Cody announced, squirming away from her.

Just as he slipped through her grasp, Wyatt caught him by the back of his shirt and hoisted him high in the air to settle on his shoulders.

"I want a ride, Dad!" Colt left Buffy and jumped on his father.

Wolf laughed.

Bill slammed his head into the timbers. Although the fence was rock solid and it would hold, Buffy hated to see Bill's head take a pounding.

"Let's go inside, shall we?" She snagged Colt halfway up Wyatt and swung him up on her own shoulders. She grunted as he landed in place. "You're huge!"

Colt leaned so suddenly that he almost tipped Buffy over forward. Colt looked her in the eye, only his head was upside down because he was leaning, vulturelike, over her. He was wearing a cowboy hat that was a miniature of his father's, and it didn't fall off. "You're strong!"

"Well, I wrestle big, ol' mean buffalo every day of my life. I had to get strong so I could whip 'em in a fair fight."

Cody said from his perch on Wyatt's shoulders, "You rassled 'em?" He spun his body around to look at Bill. He almost pitched himself off Wyatt.

Wyatt swatted him on his thigh. "Be careful up there!"

Colt leaned even farther forward until Buffy couldn't see past him. She stopped, afraid she'd walk into something.

"You really rassle buffalers? Is that how you got the name Mrs. Buffalo?"

"No, I got the name Mrs. Buffalo...uh. ... That is, my name *isn't* Mrs. Buffalo. I got the name *Buffy* because I work with buffalo all the time."

"Can we ride a buffalo like Dad did yesterday?" Cody asked.

The weight lifted off Buffy's back, and she grabbed at Colt, thinking he was falling. She saw Wolf set him solidly on the ground.

"Stay put." He reached for Cody on Wyatt's shoulders and put him beside his brother, who hadn't moved or taken his eyes off Wolf.

"No one rides a buffalo. No one." Wolf pointed his gloved hand at Bill. "No one ever gets in the pen with a buffalo. They're not pets. Every single one of them will stomp you to death if you give it half a chance. The bulls, the cows, and even the little calves."

Wolf said it with such a hard voice that both boys' eyes widened with fear. Then they turned to look at the buffalo.

Cody said a little uncertainly, "Dad would save us."

Wyatt said, "Cody!"

"Didn't you just hear what Wolf said to you?" Buffy asked fearfully.

The boys looked past Wolf at Bill. Colt took a step toward the buffalo.

"You stand right there." Wolf had their undivided attention.

Buffy glanced at Wyatt to see if he'd take exception to this treatment of his sons. Wyatt had his arms crossed and was imitating Wolf's glare—at his sons.

Cody and Colt looked at their dad and saw no help there. They turned to Buffy, and a second slow but in time, she glared at them, too.

"Look at this." Wolf bent down and jerked one boot off; then he yanked off a long gray sock and pulled up the leg of his jeans. An ugly, wicked-looking scar appeared.

"A buffalo did this to me when I was six years old. I was in a park with my family where the buffalo roamed free, and I was told to stay away from them. They seemed so tame. They just stood around eating grass. Even when I got close to them, they ignored me."

The boys looked from that vicious red scar to Wolf's serious expression.

Wolf's voice was no more than a growl. "And then I got too close. A buffalo is like that. It doesn't pay much attention to things until something gets inside its danger zone."

Cody said fearfully, "Danger zone?"

"Yes. There's this range around a buffalo that it claims for its own. With some buffalo, it's just a few feet, but with others, it can be as big as this whole ranch yard." Wolf spread his arms wide.

"So you don't know how close you can get?" Colt asked.

Wolf leaned so close to them that his voice barely carried to

Buffy's ears. "No, but you know what I think?" His voice fell further, almost to a rasping whisper. "I think they're waiting until you get close enough." Wolf shouted the last words, *"Then they get you!"*

The boys yelled and ran screaming toward Wyatt's truck.

Wolf pulled on his sock and boot; then he rolled down his pant leg and stood calmly.

Buffy raised an eyebrow and muttered, under the cover of the screaming, "That looked like a burn to me, big shot."

Wolf shrugged, "Buffalo, campfire, what's the difference?"

Wyatt said, "How'd you make them stand still like that?"

"It's a gift."

"Yeah, the gift of terrorizing children," Buffy said sarcastically.

"Bet they leave the buff alone," Wolf said smugly.

Wyatt rolled his eyes and headed for his truck.

Wolf followed along, and when the boys hopped back out, Wolf snatched Colt and settled him on his shoulders. Cody settled on top of Wyatt. They headed for the house.

Wyatt walked between Wolf and Buffy. The boys were bombarding Wolf with questions about the buffalo attack. Wolf was making up grim details that were guaranteed to keep the boys out of the buffalo pen—and probably give them nightmares besides.

Wyatt turned to Buffy, and although she'd have preferred to beg his forgiveness in private, Buffy grabbed her chance. "Wyatt, I'm—"

"I'm sorry."

At the same instant they said, "Last night I—"

They looked at each other and fell silent. Then at the same instant they said, "What did you say?"

They said nothing. The boys chattered on so there was no awkward stretch of quiet, just an awkward stretch of noise.

Buffy opened her mouth and saw Wyatt do the same. She

lifted her hand, and he stopped.

"Me first, because I'm the one who was in the wrong. I came over there on a mission of peace, and I only made things worse."

"No, you were being nice. I gave you such a hard time you finally took a swipe at me. I know you like—" He glanced upward at his wriggling son. "Just fine. You were very kind to them, and I was rude, and I'm sorry."

Buffy was determined to apologize more than he did. She'd insulted his children, for heaven's sake. "They're just normal little boys. They're perfect."

Cody swung his foot and missed kicking Buffy in the nose by a fraction of an inch.

Wyatt grabbed the marauding foot. "Yeah, right. Perfect."

Buffy glanced at the boys, not wanting them to hear themselves being discussed.

They were still grilling Wolf. Wolf was talking easily about buffalo mayhem.

"For their age, they're perfect. Even a little advanced," she said.

Wyatt's mood lifted a bit. She could see him walk a little taller, which, considering he was over six feet tall, wasn't necessary. "Yeah? You think they're advanced?"

"I do!" Buffy said stoutly. "And I'll personally help you beat up anyone who says different. Including me."

Colt said, "Are you going to beat someone up, Mrs. Buffalo?"

"Her name's Buffy," Wyatt said.

"Forget it. I kind of like Mrs. Buffalo."

"And then I had to drag myself over to the campfire," Wolf said, "and stop the bleeding by branding my leg with a burning stick."

Both boys shouted with horrified glee at the grisly story.

Sally came running out of the house. "Can I go ride the

buffalo now, Aunt Buffy?"

Wyatt looked at her with a cocky expression.

Buffy leaned forward so she could see Wolf. "You mind rolling up that pant leg again?"

"She's three," Wolf said dryly. "Her brain hasn't grown in yet. You've just got to watch her. No excuses!"

Sally jumped into Buffy's arms. Buffy wasn't ready for it, and a loud *oomph* got pounded out of her.

Wyatt said smugly, "Another perfect child."

Buffy shook her head as she swung Sally onto her shoulders. "We're hip-deep in 'em."

Jeanie stepped out of the kitchen door. She was wearing Buffy's only good pair of blue jeans. They were too long for Jeanie and about two sizes too small. She had on a blue chambray shirt, also Buffy's. But Jeanie wore it unbuttoned, tied in a knot just under her ample breasts. Her hair was perfectly curled. She had on the full array of makeup. Not a chip in sight on her nails.

Buffy had been wrestling buffalo for three hours. She no doubt looked and smelled like it. Buffy's teeth clicked together.

Wyatt glanced at her then focused on Jeanie. "Hello. We met briefly yesterday."

"Call me Jeanie," she purred. Then, like it was a question that had fascinated millions of people for millions of years, she asked, "And you are?"

Wyatt lifted his Stetson off his head. That showed good manners. He hadn't so much as doffed it for Buffy. "Wyatt. Wyatt Shaw. I'm your closest neighbor."

Jeanie came down the steps of the porch that wrapped all the way around the white two-story farmhouse. She moved with the graceful flow of prairie grass in a summer wind. Her eyes never left Wyatt. "And you are the man who saved us yesterday. You rode in here like a knight in shining armor and saved all of us."

Cody and Colt both overreacted to the reminder of their father's heroism. They started trying to climb down from their lofty seats. Wolf and Wyatt set them down, and they rushed toward the house, yelling the story back and forth.

Sally squirmed to be free, and Buffy let her go. "Wait for me!" She disappeared into the house after the boys.

Jeanie came forward and slipped between Buffy and Wyatt. Since there really wasn't room, she had to get really close to Wyatt.

Buffy had to back off or run her older sister over. She didn't make the decision lightly.

Jeanie looped her hand around Wyatt's elbow until his arm was hugged against her body. She said in a throaty voice that Buffy had only heard her use on men, "Come in and let me thank you properly."

Buffy stumbled slightly at the suggestive tone of voice and was left behind. As near as she could tell, neither Wyatt nor Jeanie noticed, although Wolf gave her a strange look.

Wyatt and Jeanie went into the house, and Wolf followed along.

Buffy had a stricken moment. She almost turned and went back to the buffalo. It was ten thirty. She had eight hours of work to do before noon. Then her day really started.

She crossed her arms and thought of her sister feeding Wyatt the coffee Buffy had ferreted out of the pantry and made earlier this morning. Not a box had been unpacked yet, unless Buffy had done it. She wondered if Jeanie could find where Buffy had put the coffee mugs.

If Jeanie found them, she'd look cool and competent, something Buffy hadn't ever managed in her life. If Jeanie couldn't find the cups, she'd look flustered and helpless. She'd give Wyatt her poor-little-old-me look, and he'd jump in to slay the pesky Dragon of Missing Stoneware.

Annoyed at herself, Buffy marched into the kitchen. She'd drink one cup of coffee, but that was all. She needed to get back to work. Mostly she just needed to get out of here.

four

He needed to get back to work. But mostly he just needed to get out of here.

Wyatt clung to his patience. He needed just a few seconds to talk to the Buffalo Gal, say his pathetic apologies, and then he'd go. He had three days' worth of work to finish today.

And this little blond airhead wouldn't quit chirping at him.

Just when he thought he might implode, Buffy erupted from her kitchen chair. "I can't sit around here chitchatting all morning." She seemed to spread her accusation of laziness evenly between Blondie and himself. "Some of us have work to do." She stormed out.

Wolf got up like the oak kitchen chair had an ejector seat. "Yep, got work. Gotta go." He ran as if Wyatt was going to whip out a doily and insist they sip a cup of tea.

Wyatt stood and clapped his hat on his head.

Blondie latched both of her hands on his forearm and hung on with a grip that belied her dainty size. "No, don't go. I was hoping I'd have a minute to thank you properly for saving Sally."

Wyatt was ready to use straight force on her to get her to turn loose.

The boys chose that moment to race through the kitchen as they had done with extreme regularity. This time they skidded into Blondie and smashed her into him. She flung her arms around him, and just like that, the boys were gone, fighting some war or other, Sally hot on their heels.

Buffy was pulling her gloves off her hands as she came in. "I need you to move your—" Her boots clumped to a stop, and her jaw dropped open then snapped shut. He'd heard her teeth *click* like that before. It wasn't a good sign.

Wyatt pried the octopus off him. "I'll move it."

"No, really. You're obviously busy," she said coldly. "Just give me your keys."

He walked up to her, and she did some quick surgery on him with her laser eyeballs. He knew exactly why. He'd have been mad if he'd walked in on her with some man. And that made no sense, so he refused to think about it.

"The keys are in it. I've got to get going."

"Whatever." Buffy left the kitchen.

Wyatt followed, hot on Buffy's heels.

Jeanie caught up to him. "I'd love to come over and see what you're doing with the boys' room. I'll drive myself over one of these evenings." She ran one hand up his sleeve. "Thanks for asking."

Wyatt recalled the boys shouting about painting the color of Sally's T-shirt over the ugly pink. Colt had yelled that it was going to be bloodred. Not true. He'd gone with off-white. Whatever she'd heard about the painting, he was absolutely clear on asking her to come over. . . .

He hadn't.

"Don't come without calling first. We're gone almost all the time." He unhooked her claws.

The boys dashed past him. He grabbed a couple of handfuls of them and towed them along screaming. He lugged both boys and saw Buffy was coming along.

"We're gone almost all the time?" She snorted and veered off toward that stupid, worthless buffalo.

He still hadn't had that moment alone with her. He couldn't let the boys go—he might never catch 'em again. And the leech in the kitchen might get him again. Finally in complete frustration, he yelled after Buffy, "You know I came over here to apologize to you."

That froze her in her tracks. She turned around and wrinkled her brow. "What did you do that requires an apology?"

Wyatt looked at his boys, avidly listening as they swung, one from each of his arms. He arched his eyebrows at her, hoping she'd get that he couldn't talk. "Surely I've done something you can think of."

Buffy smirked.

"You told me you were sorry last night," he said.

"What was she sorry for, Dad?" Colt asked, dangling from his arm and wrapping his feet boa constrictor–like around Wyatt's leg.

"I imagine she's sorry for almost every second she's spent in my company."

Cody walked up Wyatt's body until he was hanging upside down. The kid was one prehensile tail and an opposable thumb away from being a spider monkey.

"That's so true," Buffy said in a snippy voice.

"Sometimes I'm sorry I have to hang around with myself."

"I'll bet that's right." He caught a little smile on her lips.

Cody's feet swung past Wyatt's face. "I'm hanging around you, Dad. And I'm not sorry."

Wyatt wondered ruefully if she was having any second thoughts about insulting his boys.

Colt picked that moment to let go with one hand and try to pry Cody's hands loose from Wyatt's arm. Cody held on desperately and managed to kick Wyatt in the face while he was battling for his handhold.

Sally came screaming out of the house at that minute and slammed into Buffy's legs. Buffy hoisted her up and ran a gentle hand over her head. "I'm the one who should be apologizing."

Wyatt got kicked again and lowered both boys to the ground

by crouching. He still didn't let them go. He looked at both of them wriggling in the dirt like a couple of sidewinders. "You asked me to forgive you, and like a jerk, I wouldn't," Wyatt said. "God gave me a little reminder later that He's forgiven me a lot."

"Oh, surely not." Buffy arched her brows too innocently.

"And I know I was being rude until I deserved to be slugged. A lesser woman would have been pounding on me by that time."

Buffy did smile this time; then she sobered. "Instead, I took a potshot at the most precious, innocent thing in your life." She hugged Sally tighter. "I've spent my life working with buffalo."

"You're twenty-five. What life? You're a baby."

"And how old were you again?"

Wyatt shrugged.

"I had my first summer job at a park when I was twelve. I cleaned out stalls that held injured buffalo."

"You hauled manure?"

"Yeah, pretty much. Did I mention they didn't pay me?"

"You hauled manure for free?"

"I'd have done anything to work with those buffalo. I was forbidden to get near them of course, but I did everything they'd allow, and they had a tight budget so they let me do a lot. I've been at it for thirteen years. The fire department lets you retire after twenty."

"Well, your buffalo aren't on fire, so you'll probably have to keep at it till you're sixty-five."

"I've taken every class, every job, every chance I could get to be around them. When I leave here, it's for Yellowstone. It's got the finest management system in the world. And I'm going to be in charge. You don't think they'd let a novice take the manager's job here, do you? I'm an expert."

"Okay, you've been working with buffalo almost as long as

I've been ranching. I started almost as soon as I could walk."

"I'm better with buffalo than I am with people." She gave Sally a noisy kiss on her chubby neck.

Sally giggled.

Buffy smiled at her, and Wyatt had a hard time taking his eyes off that smile.

"I've got a long way to go in learning manners. The things I said to you about them"—Buffy glanced at his boys—"were unforgivable."

"You know, I had the same thought myself," Wyatt admitted. "Did I mention the little reminder? Of all I'd been forgiven? I wouldn't be much of a Christian if I didn't forgive you."

"If you really came over here for that"—she glanced past his shoulder again toward the house—"then you're a very nice man. I accept your apology and hope you accept mine."

"Already did," Wyatt said.

"I was going to drive over as soon as Bill had been turned loose. I thought we should give starting over one more chance."

"Yeah, well just remember who went first."

Buffy smiled again then hesitantly said, "My sister. . ."

"What about Mommy, Aunt Buffy? Did Mommy do something again? Are we going to have to move again?"

Buffy gasped. "No, sweetie. Your mommy's fine, and she never did anything that made us move. I don't want you to think that."

"But once I heard you say—"

Buffy laid her hand gently over Sally's mouth. Sally couldn't know that her mother had made some pretty shady friends back in Oklahoma, after Michael had run off. They hadn't made this move because of that, but Buffy had been glad to leave behind some bad influences.

She turned to Wyatt. "I'd better get back to work. Are we even on the apologies now?"

"Dead even, I'd say." The boys made a sudden concerted break for freedom, and only six years of hard-learned lessons kept Wyatt one step ahead of them.

"Then maybe we should never speak to each other again," she said.

Wyatt thought she sounded kind of sad.

"Quit while we're ahead?" he suggested.

"Something like that."

Wolf shouted from across the yard, "I'm ready to load the old bull. I can use a hand, Buffy."

"We'd better get out of your way," Wyatt said.

He saw Buffy look past Wolf to the buffalo, and he felt her attention drawing toward the big animals. Her heart wasn't in it when she gathered herself and turned back to him. She looked down at Sally and tried to be diplomatic, "Anyway, she's been known to. . ."

Wyatt saw the trust in that baby girl's blue eyes and knew Buffy still wanted to say something about Jeanie but couldn't in front of Sally.

Buffy was helpless against that look. She shrugged again and said, "Uh. . .over—"

Jeanie came to the door behind Wyatt. She'd lost that breathy, dumb blond voice and now spoke in a tone that made the hair on the back of his neck stand straight up. "Buffy, when are you going to get some groceries? There's nothing in the house to eat. Why do I always have to— Oh, hi, Wyatt." The crooning voice was back. He heard her jogging down the porch steps.

Wyatt gave Buffy a wild look.

"She's been known to. . .you might say. . .over-depend." With the tiniest possible trace of malice, Buffy added, "I suspect depending on you will do as well as depending on me."

Wyatt shuddered at the thought. "Well, gotta go. We're late. Let's get out of here, boys." He scooped the boys up, one per arm, and held them like a human shield as he practically ran for his truck. He couldn't see any one of the three women for the cloud of dust he left behind. But as the road curved away from the Buffalo Commons, he saw Buffy striding toward the buffalo pen, tugging on her leather gloves.

five

Buffy woke to the crack of thunder.

She jerked awake and was already getting dressed without taking a second to try and figure out what was going on. Whatever it was, she wanted to face it with her boots on.

The thunder rumbled again, and she was running down the steps toward the kitchen, when she heard Wolf yelling for all he was worth. The only word she could make out was "stampede." She didn't need to hear more.

She met Wolf at the back door. A ball of lightning split the night, and an explosion rang far across the black sky. A flare of fire could be seen in the distance.

Wolf turned away from the blaze. "That last bolt of lightning set a tree on fire. The herd is already running. We've got to get out there."

Buffy ran for her truck. She shouted at her rapidly moving hired men, "Someone take a couple of rigs around the outside of the fence. If you can beat them to the end of the pasture, honk and flash your headlights. That might head them off. If they hit that fence running this hard, they could knock it down."

"I'll drive myself," Wolf shouted over the howling wind. "We might need every truck on the place."

Buffy had the truck started and floored before she got the door shut. In just two weeks at the Buffalo Commons, she was on her second mad scramble across the prairie.

&

Wyatt jerked out of a sound sleep.

He'd never felt an earthquake before, but he was feeling one now. Then a second later, he knew better. Stampede!

He yanked on his pants, jammed his feet into his boots, grabbed his shirt, and was already dressed and running by the time he was fully awake. He ran past Anna, who came stumbling out of her room. He skidded to a stop and grabbed her arm so hard he knew she'd be bruised tomorrow. "I'm going to get the boys. You stay up here. The herd is out. They're stampeding around the house."

"The cattle?" Anna asked. "The cattle have never stampeded before, Uncle Wyatt. And you don't have the herd on any pasture around here, do you?"

Bright flashes of lightning glared out the upstairs window. "The storm must have set them off." He was already down the stairs, his boots clumping on each step, his unbuttoned shirt flying.

Bodies crashed against the house, which shook on its foundation. The deafening noise drowned out everything.

He dashed into the boys' room in time to see Cody running for a window. Wyatt sprinted across the room, grabbed his son, and lifted him. Colt was only a step behind his brother, and Wyatt managed to grab him, too, then turn to the window in time to have it shatter in his face. He shoved the boys behind his back as flying glass slit his skin.

A huge head slammed through. A buffalo head.

The boys screamed. Wyatt staggered and backed away, clinging to his sons.

The big beast let out a strangled, roaring bellow. One front leg came through into the room. The animal kicked as if to tear out the wall and run all of them down. Then, with a plaintive bawl of pain, the buffalo pulled its head back and thundered across his porch.

Wyatt, with a son in each arm, ran to the window, his feet crunching on countless shards of glass. Another buffalo ran past his window so close he could have slapped it.

Cody reached out one hand, and Wyatt took a quick step back. The buffalo got past, and he saw more of them. More and more. Everywhere. His high-powered yard lights lit up a boiling sea of coarse brown fur and bobbing horns. He heard the bellow of frantic animals. Hundreds of them. Maybe thousands.

The three poles that held his yard lights began quivering as they took one hard hit after another. They began teetering then swaying. One at a time, in a shower of sparks, they fell. One landed on the beautiful old barn built by his grandfather at the turn of the century.

Wyatt watched in horror as flames began to flicker in the haymow. Forcing himself to look away from the destruction, he whirled and ran with the boys up the steps to Anna. "Hang on to them. None of you come down!"

He raced back to the living room and gripped the edge of the window to keep from running for the barn to fight the fire. Running out into that raging herd was certain death.

He saw headlights, still a mile away, following the herd. The car was coming out of a field, not the road. A flare of lightning lit up the yard, and he saw the fence around the horse corral trampled under massive hooves. Gumby ran wild with the buffalo; then, just as another blaze of lightning exploded overhead, the horse stumbled. Wyatt couldn't see if Gumby stayed on his feet or not.

"No, boys," Anna yelled. "Get back here."

"Dad? We want to watch." Cody came charging down the stairs. Wyatt realized the boy wore nothing but gym shorts. Colt was right behind him, running straight for the glass-coated floor in his bare feet.

Wyatt turned on his sons. "Get back up those stairs and stay there."

Cody froze on the spot. Wyatt had never heard that sound from his own mouth. It was an order no one—man, woman, or child—would ever disobey. Cody and Colt whirled around and dashed back up the stairs.

Wyatt turned back to the window and saw the flaming roof of his barn. It stood away from his steel machine shed, but sparks raised to the sky toward his house. If the house caught fire, they had to run outside. . . .

Wyatt began to pray. He felt as if he were falling. Sinking back into the past.

The herd came and came and came. He'd heard stories of buffalo herds on the prairie. Herds so large the whole world was alive with them. They spread from one end of the horizon to the other.

"Dear God, what's going on? Don't let anyone be hurt."

He thought of Buffy and wondered if they'd overrun her place first. He imagined Buffy crushed beyond recognition under thousands of hooves. He knew she'd never let this happen if she could humanly prevent it. What had happened?

"Dear God, let them be all right."

There were more homes on down the road. They weren't that far from the little town of Cold Creek. How many people might die before these beasts stopped their stampede? He thought of Bill. One buffalo, alone, running wild. He hadn't been easy to bring down. How did anyone ever round up a herd this size? They trampled everything, and still they came.

He fumbled for the phone, not knowing whom he'd call. Buffy? 911? The line was dead.

He heard the crashing and brawling of the huge bodies blundering through his farm equipment, his outbuildings. His barn was reduced nearly to ashes already, but nothing else had caught. A gust of wind whooshed over the barn, and sparks flew. Wyatt heard a soft *whumph* and saw his truck start to burn. A ruptured gas tank, maybe? A spark from the barn or a sharp hoof? Anna's car went next.

Then his own internal gas tank ruptured. He went tearing for the back of the house and his locked gun cabinet. He was so mad he couldn't remember where he'd left the key for a few minutes. He finally got it open, then had to load it, and then had to lock the cabinet back up. How had John Wayne ever gotten anything done?

He ran back to his broken window and—nothing. They were gone. The splinters of glass and the gaping window were proof they had been here. Choking dust filled the air and covered everything in the house. But only a rumble of faraway hooves marked their passing. He wanted to sit down. He wanted to collapse.

He wanted to shoot a buffalo.

He cocked his rifle and stormed out of the house. A wind that drove the storm clouds high overhead caught at his shirt as he ran down the wrecked steps of his porch. He couldn't drive after the herd because his truck and Anna's car were destroyed.

Buffy came flying into the yard in her rig. She slammed on the brakes when she saw him and leaned over to throw open the passenger door. "Are you all right?" she asked frantically. "Did anyone get hurt?"

Wyatt heard the needle-sharp edge of hysteria in her voice. "We're all right. My ranch is destroyed, and my livestock are all dead or run off, but the kids and I are fine."

He was as close to being in a killing fury as a man could be.

She took a wild look at his rifle as if she wondered if he'd use it on her then glanced at his face. "You're bleeding!" She scrambled across the seat and stood in front of him.

He looked down at his bare chest and saw rivulets of blood streaming down. He wiped his sleeve over his face, and it came away red. He did a quick inventory of his wounds then buttoned his shirt. "They're just scratches. A buffalo tried to climb through my living room window. It's nothing." His tone of voice could have burned a barn down on its own, no buffalo stampede required.

"It's not nothing." Buffy checked him over, her callused hands gentle on him.

He didn't want to like this female softness. . .but he did.

She dabbed at his face then pulled a handkerchief out of her pocket and dabbed some more. At last she was satisfied. "None of them are deep. You'll be all right. I've got to get after the herd."

"Don't move. I'm going with you, but I can't leave the boys."

"I've got to go," Buffy shouted.

Wyatt forgot all about her gentle touch. He grabbed her arm. "You owe me. You wait right here."

Buffy looked in his eyes then gave a short nod of her head.

"Buffy, this is Wolf. Come in. I've got the sheriff on his way, and I've called everyone I can think of to come help. I've got a shipment of tranquilizers coming by helicopter. Mr. Leonard is pulling out all the stops. No expense spared."

Wyatt nearly ripped the passenger's side door open and grabbed the handset of Buffy's CB radio. "That's because he knows he's going to get sued until his ears bleed."

"That you, Wyatt?" Wolf asked.

"It's me."

"What happened at your place?" Wolf sounded exhausted.

"We all lived. But they took everything on the place except the house. They're a menace, Wolf. I've been telling you that from the first."

"It's not the fault of those buffalo. If lightning stampeded your cattle, they could do just as much damage."

"They never have, and you know it." Wyatt dropped his head

into his hands, trying to get hold of himself.

Buffy took the mike. "The buffalo are following Wyatt's lane out to the road. The herd is running straight north. They can't run much farther without tiring. Call the rest of the men and tell them to try again to get ahead of them."

"When we first brought them into the country," Wolf said, "we held them in some pens just south of Cold Creek. That holding area is still there. If we could get them stopped, then maybe we could toss them some hay and lead them to it."

"You know how they follow your truck when you drive out and throw bales?" Buffy asked.

"Yeah, once they've calmed down, that might work. We could lead them into the pen and load them from there."

"How far to the pen?"

Wyatt was suddenly in possession of the CB again. "I know where it is. I'll give her directions. There'll be stragglers, Wolf. You'll never get them in one sweep."

"No, but we can cut the odds in our favor real quick."

"And the stragglers will be in every herd in the area. It might take weeks to round them up. Every rancher around here could lose their whole herd."

"Mr. Leonard will make it right, Wyatt," Wolf said quietly. "You won't be out anything."

"Money," Wyatt snarled. "That's your answer to everything."

Buffy wrestled him for the mike. Because he wasn't prepared, she got it. She clicked the TALK button. "Make it happen, Wolf. I'm going to make sure Wyatt's family is safe; then I'll follow the buffalo and keep tabs on them. Open up that holding pen. Get the hay you need. I'll let Wyatt yell at me while I'm trailing the herd."

"I can take it, Buffy. This has been between Wyatt and me from the first."

"I know. But you've got work to do."

Wyatt clenched his teeth until she hung up. "You don't need to talk about me like I'm another chore that has to be finished. If you think—"

"See to your family, Wyatt. Can Anna drive herself over to my place? She and the boys can stay with Jeanie and Sally."

Wyatt looked at the wreckage of his place. "What are they supposed to drive?" But even when he said it, he knew. "I'll be right back."

He turned and ran toward the house. He stumbled to a stop over the body of a baby buffalo. He saw it had been crushed to death, run over by the herd. He dropped to one knee even as he recognized the contradiction of the rifle clutched in his hand. He felt the compassion every rancher has for creatures who die before their time. He turned wearily to Buffy. "You lost a calf."

He heard her gasp.

He strode into the house. "Anna!"

Anna appeared at the head of the stairs. She and the boys were fully dressed. "Are you hurt, Uncle Wyatt? You're bleeding."

"The cuts aren't deep. The bleeding has already stopped."

Anna accepted it better than Buffy had. "I saw it from up here. Is the old pickup in the machine shed?"

That was exactly what Wyatt had in mind. Anna had lived with him for four summers now. She'd learned to drive on that old truck. "Take it over to the Buffalo Commons. You can sleep there. I don't think the house is going to burn. The barn has died down."

"And my car," Anna added bitterly.

Wyatt looked again and saw tears had left tracks in the dirt on Anna's face. Dust covered everything and everyone. Wyatt couldn't imagine the effort it was going to take to clean up this mess.

"And the Buffalo Commons house is fine?" Anna asked, her voice laced with anger. "The buffalo didn't hurt their place?"

Wyatt didn't like the settled look of hatred on Anna's face. He wondered if his face looked the same. He tried to control himself for her sake and the boys'. "I just had the old truck going yesterday. It'll start up. Let's get you out of here."

Anna gave a tense nod of her head. "But I think I'll go over to the Swensons'." She mentioned an elderly couple who ranched about ten miles to the west. "I'd just as soon stay there."

"I don't want you driving that way, Anna. The herd may have fanned out in that direction. You could find out the Swensons had their own stampede. You could be walking from the truck to the house and get attacked by one of the big brutes. The one place we know the buffalo *are not* is the Commons."

"Fine," Anna said sullenly. "We'll go there. . .at least until morning."

"Thanks. I want you out of here before I leave, in case of fire."

They went out the door and saw Buffy kneeling beside the buffalo calf. Anna walked past the calf and Buffy without speaking. The boys, subdued for once, stared wide-eyed at the baby. Wyatt kept them moving.

When he had them loaded in the truck, he said to a white-faced Anna, "Be careful. The herd is past us, but there might be stragglers. Don't drive fast in case one would jump out in front of you."

"A little worse than that deer you hit last spring," Anna said with vicious sarcasm.

"If something happens—a flat tire or anything—stay in the truck until someone comes to help you." Wyatt patted her awkwardly on the shoulder. "Your cell phone won't work out here, but you've got a CB in there, so call for help if you need it." He added, "We'll get your car fixed, honey. It's insured. It'll be okay."

Anna twisted her lips in something that was a horrible imitation of a smile. "And that makes it right? This nightmare?"

Anna's voice began rising in delayed panic. "What if the boys had gotten outside?"

Wyatt knew she was right. Cody and Colt couldn't resist getting out to see what the ruckus was.

"They'd have been killed," Anna said in a hoarse whisper that Wyatt knew the boys, who were hanging on every word, had to hear.

"But they weren't, honey. Just go."

Anna nodded, clenching her jaw to keep from saying more.

Wyatt watched as the truck drove away. Then he turned back to Buffy, who'd returned to her truck. Wyatt climbed in beside her. "Let's go find your buffalo."

"Are you planning to use that thing?" She tipped her head at the rifle Wyatt still had clenched in his rigid hand.

"If I have to."

Buffy drove.

For a while, the silence in the cab was so thick Wyatt could barely inhale. But he wasn't going to apologize again. He was already over his quota for the year.

Buffy pointed straight ahead. "There's one of them." The buffalo was still kicking up its heels. It ran full out tirelessly, as if it could go on forever.

"How far to the pens?" Buffy asked.

"It's at least ten miles. If they decide to quit running, Wolf'll never get them to walk that far as a herd. They'll just start spreading out and foraging."

"Ten miles." Buffy sounded hopeless as they drew closer to the running animal. "They've already been running longer than that from the Commons. But buffalo can lope along for hours. They might keep going most of the way."

Wyatt could see more of them ahead.

"Are there any more ranch houses between here and there?" Buffy asked.

"None on a direct path. There's a country school about three miles to the east, but it's on the other side of Cold Creek. And there's a country church on past the pens, the one the boys and I attend. If we don't stop them, they'll probably ruin that." Wyatt watched more buffalo appear in the headlights. "But they'll miss both those things if Wolf can lead them to the holding pens. They'll need to be turned a little to the east after a while, but there's a steep bank along the creek if they keep on this course. That'll turn 'em, I hope. If they were still stampeding, they'd probably go right over it, and most of them wouldn't survive, but if they've slowed by then, it'll turn 'em naturally."

He heard the lift in his voice. He was getting involved in the project of recapturing the buffalo. That was the nature of ranching. If something got out, you got it in. If your neighbor had trouble, you pitched in to make it right.

With a resigned sigh, he knew he had no other choice. His rifle was useless unless they were attacked by a single buffalo. He'd calmed down enough to know shooting them wouldn't solve the problem. "A buffalo commons," he said coldly.

"What?" Buffy looked away from her prey.

"That was your plan, wasn't it? To turn the whole state of South Dakota into unfenced prairie? Give it back to the buffalo?"

"Well, it's the way nature planned it."

"And God had another plan, didn't He? He made man. He gave him dominion over the animals. Or are you one of those people who throw out the parts of the Bible that don't suit you?"

"I don't throw out parts of the Bible. I can show respect for the planet and still be a Christian. People who think animal rights are in conflict with human rights just aren't trying to adapt. Destroying one species after another endangers us all. And a person can live a healthy life without meat in his diet."

Wyatt turned on her furiously. "You know that might be true in America. This is a rich country, and we have a million options in our diet, but if it's immoral to eat meat here, then it's immoral everywhere. What about the people in Africa who have one herd of goats for the whole village? What if that's their only food. Are you really going to tell them they're sinners for eating that goat? Are you going to tell a man his children have to starve to death because an animal has the same right to life a human being has?"

"Don't try to compare—"

"So it's a sin here," Wyatt said sarcastically. "Animals have the right to life, liberty, and the pursuit of happiness in America. But in Africa, well, that's different. Eat up. Your ethics are pretty convenient for you. Sin is now a matter of geography."

"I don't know why you keep talking about sin. It's not about sin."

"I thought you said animals have rights. If that's true, then they have the right to life. I can no more eat a chicken than I can eat one of my kids."

"That's disgusting." Buffy dropped the speed of her truck again as the buffalo in front of her slowed.

"What's disgusting is you putting those dangerous animals on a par with human life. You know everyone talks about saving the tiger. They talk about how elephants and rhinos are disappearing from the wild. Well, let me tell you something, Buffalo Gal, I'd be a real poor sport about my son being eaten by a tiger. It's so easy for you to sit here, thousands of miles away, and talk about leaving large, dangerous animals in the wild, but the reality of living in a village that is in the hunting territory of a pride of lions is pretty grim.

"Do you think those poachers who shoot elephants for their tusks don't want them dead and gone? Do you think I want a herd of buffalo rampaging through my ranch? Do you think I want wolves and mountain lions roaming my land? Is there any way for me to relax and appreciate them when my children are at risk every time they step out the door?"

Wyatt rubbed his hand over his mouth to keep from saying any more. His other hand tightened on his rifle, which rested beside his thigh, the muzzle pointed toward the floor of the truck. He stared at the buffalo in front of them.

An occasional flash of lightning showed the earth, a living mass of movement in the distance.

Buffy said in a low, urgent voice, "There may be some fanatics who really believe a rat has as much right to life as I do, but I'm not one of them."

Wyatt raised his hands as if in surrender. It didn't look much like surrender with the rifle in his left hand. He tried to quit sounding like a madman. "I'm yelling at you, and I know this isn't your fault. And I know Mr. Leonard has tried. I've seen the efforts he's gone to. He's supported this area in a lot of ways. But that doesn't change the basic argument, does it? I'll believe in animal rights when I see a chimpanzee judge put a cat in prison for killing a mouse."

"Wyatt, now's not the time to talk about this. You're upset, and I don't blame you. I'm going to insist that Mr. Leonard raise the budget to include riders to patrol the fence night and day. We need a stronger fence. You'll see, we—"

"We won't see about anything. I won't rest until those buffalo get out of this area. You know, if you want to restore this area to its natural state and make a real buffalo commons, Leonard needs a predator for the food chain. He wants to reintroduce wolves into the area. Mountain lions. Grizzly bears. You think a wolf is going to face a buffalo when he can have one of my calves? But it doesn't matter, because I'll be long gone if Mr. Leonard has his way. What a harebrained scheme. What arrogance. What disrespect for me and my neighbors." Wyatt forced himself to be silent again.

"You know how badly I feel about this."

Now that they were close enough to hear the thundering hooves of the herd, he flashed back to that buffalo smashing through his living room window. He saw his boys running into that glass-strewed carpet. He saw his horse go down. He rubbed his hand into his hair, and glass cut his hand. He opened the window to shake off the glass. Dirt billowed into the truck, stirred up by the herd, so he closed it again.

Buffy drove along, tailing the stragglers. There was a kind of desperate stillness to her, as if she didn't want to attract his attention and start him yelling again.

Wyatt tried to let go of his rage. "I'm sorry. I know this isn't your fault. I know you've had as much harm done to you as I have with this mess." He didn't mean it, but he said it.

"We spend way too much time apologizing to each other."

"I've noticed."

"Look, they're veering off east."

Sure enough, they were. They were slowing down, too. The gravel road that led to the pens was the path of least resistance, and they followed it.

"They probably built this road on a trail left by buffalo," Buffy said.

"It's the low road. It winds around the hills and avoids the creeks."

"Just like a buffalo would."

Wyatt didn't respond.

The buffalo in front of them dropped from its ground-eating lope into a rugged trot. It moved along for a mile or so at that speed and then fell to a walk.

Buffy stopped the truck, and they sat, listening to the thundering hooves fade as the rest of the herd began to walk. Silence reigned. They passed through the dust kicked up by the running herd, and the air cleared as they drove slowly onward.

The lightning storm faded in the distance.

"We'll make this right." Buffy turned to him. "I promise. Even if I have to work at your ranch single-handedly until everything is rebuilt and replaced. I'm so thankful none of you were hurt." She'd pulled the truck to a stop in the middle of the road but left it running, and he could see her in the dim light of the dashboard.

She reached out and touched his temple and pulled away a finger tipped in blood. "At least not hurt badly. And no matter what I say about animal rights, the danger we put your family in is inexcusable. We're going to do whatever it takes to make sure this never happens again. You have my word on that."

Buffy was asking for his forgiveness. . .again.

The night closed around them. The whole world was silent. Not a cricket chirped. Not a frog croaked. They'd all been scared away by the monsters crashing through their territory.

Wyatt turned to look at the strolling herd, disappearing out of the beam of their headlights. His head dropped back against the headrest. "I believe you, Buffy. But I don't want to live with this kind of threat in my backyard. And I don't know any other life. I have to fight for my ranch, and that means the buffalo have to go." He remembered Anna's words. He wondered if she'd first heard them from him. "There are some things Mr. Leonard's money can't fix."

"And if the buffalo go, I go with them," Buffy said.

Wyatt hadn't thought of that. Buffy and Wolf and a couple dozen other hands at the Buffalo Commons. Mr. Leonard was one of the area's largest employers. He paid well, too. Full-time jobs with good benefits—something rare out here. Wyatt hired some help during the haying season, but otherwise his ranch was a one-man operation. Most ranches were.

He looked at her in the gentle light of the dashboard. Her light brown eyes glowed with regret. "Where would you go?" he asked.

"I don't know. I'm supposed to spend three months here is all. Then, when my doctoral dissertation is done, I've got a job waiting for me in Yellowstone. It's the premier buffalo herd in the nation, at least to my way of thinking. I want to spend a few years there, learning everything I can. Then I thought I might try to get on with Mr. Leonard permanently. He's doing the most exciting work with buffalo of anyone. Of course if this blows up in his face, he'll have to abandon it. He has ranches like this all over the country." With a sad little laugh, she added, "There's not a lot of call for a buffalo specialist."

"Who was your guidance counselor in high school?" Wyatt asked. "You could have used some career counseling."

"Actually, I'm a licensed veterinarian."

That brought Wyatt's head up. "A veterinarian? I thought you said you were twenty-five."

Buffy shrugged. "What can I say? I'm gifted."

"We could use a veterinarian."

"But I specialized in buffalo. I didn't learn much else." She rested her cheek against her headrest.

Wyatt knew she wasn't talking about buffalo. What she didn't learn much about were men, sitting too close to her in dark trucks. Then he saw his boys running for the window and his barn collapsing. There was always going to be a big, fat, ugly buffalo standing squarely between them. "Why buffalo? Whatever possessed you to be obsessed with those nasty, stupid critters?"

Just that easily, the spell between them was broken. But so was most of the tension.

Buffy leaned away from him and smiled. "They're no uglier than cows."

"Sure they are. Way uglier. A cow's a pretty little thing."

"That's why a woman is so tickled when someone calls her a cow."

"All the women I say it to are honored."

"Try calling one a heifer sometime and see if she likes it."

"Already have. I've had some luck with it."

Buffy laughed. "Well, that just goes to show. . ."

"What?"

She gripped the steering wheel. "An hour ago, when I realized that the herd was loose and headed for your place, when I realized you and your family could be killed by the buffalo, I was so scared I would have bet I'd never laugh again."

Wyatt heard more in her voice than the worry of a rancher for her neighbor. He heard the same thing he'd heard that morning two weeks ago when she hadn't liked finding him with Jeanie. The same thing he'd heard behind every insult and apology. There couldn't be anything between them. . .but there was.

Without making a conscious choice, Wyatt reached for her and pulled her into his arms. She looked startled, but she let him drag her over to his side of the truck.

Wyatt, knowing every move was pure stupid, lowered his head.

Lights in the rearview mirror jerked them apart.

Buffy scooted away from him so quickly, Wyatt thought she'd been snagged by a lasso and hog-tied to her door.

Before Wyatt could say anything, Wolf pulled up on Wyatt's side of the truck, and Wyatt opened his window in a night so full of dust he could chew the air.

"I'm just going to ease on through the herd." Wolf jerked his chin in a nod. "They usually let me drive right out among 'em. I'm hoping they'll catch the scent of the hay."

Seth called out from the back end. "If they don't follow, I'll throw out a little hay to bait 'em. The sheriff is already waiting at the pen. He'll have it open, and he's lined up every truck he could muster to form a wall, including several semis. We're hoping they'll all just walk right in; then we'll load 'em and take 'em home."

"Not all," Wyatt said.

"Nope." Wolf shook his dark head. "I already saw a few turned aside from the herd. I've been radioing their locations to the other hands, and they're darting them with the tranquilizer gun and picking them up. We'll get 'em, Wyatt. You know we will."

"I know you'll try. But how many of my cows will be pregnant with buff calves by then? It's the height of breeding season right now. And if your buffalo have brucellosis, my herd may have to be quarantined and slaughtered."

"We'll replace them if it happens," Wolf said. "It's the best we can do."

Wyatt's hand, resting against the open window frame, clenched into a fist. "It's not good enough."

"I know." Wolf began driving forward. He was the kind of man Wyatt could understand. Now wasn't the time for talking. Now was the time for doing. Wolf, like Wyatt, kept going forward because there was no other direction a man could go.

"You stay back here, Buffy. We need someone to bring up the rear." Wolf drove into the slowly moving herd.

Wyatt saw the buffalo perk up their heads as Wolf drove by. "They know him," he said with quiet amazement.

"He sings to them. Listen. It sounds like an old Indian chant of some kind."

He heard the low, guttural crooning of a Native American tribal song. The buffalo started falling into line behind the truck. Wyatt said, "They know their master's voice."

"We should all be so wise," Buffy said.

six

"That would be stupid!" Wyatt turned from watching the tenth semi pull away from the stock pens.

Buffy was sick of being called names. She jammed her hands on her hips. "We need to call the radio station. The newspapers. The television stations. We need to *warn* people, for heaven's sake!"

"The nearest paper is in Hot Springs, and it only comes out once a week. There's no TV station that carries local news. If Rapid City got the story, it would just be for the sake of gossip. What can they do? And as for the radio letting people know, we already did."

"Called the radio?" Buffy asked.

"Let people know. Wolf phoned everyone in the area hours ago."

Buffy nodded. "Makes sense."

"They're all taking precautions with their families, and they're riding out at first light to spot runaways. They'll start phoning in reports of buffalo as soon as they spot them."

"That's the last of 'em," Wolf said.

Buffy hadn't given much thought to Wolf's age before tonight, but now she noticed the gray hairs reflected by the headlights. His face was lined with fatigue.

Of course, she might have gray hair and lines in her face after tonight, too. "Did you get a head count, Wolf?" Buffy had stopped pacing for a while as she watched the buffalo load, but now she went back to it. She was running on pure adrenaline, and she needed to keep moving or start screaming.

"I counted every semiload, and we're putting each load in a separate pen back at the Commons. We'll recount there. We started this night with 1,462, including the spring calves."

"I didn't know the herd had gotten so big," Wyatt said with obvious disapproval.

He was the one she'd start screaming at if she cracked, so she kept her mouth clamped shut. He'd been growing increasingly rude. He responded to every comment with terse insults. She didn't know how much more of it she could take.

"I've loaded 1,241 on the trailers. We kept careful count."

"Two hundred and twenty-one buffalo missing." Wyatt bristled with hostility.

Buffy couldn't blame him, but that didn't keep her from wanting to stuff a cork in his mouth. And unfortunately it didn't keep her from thinking about him almost kissing her and, worse yet, her almost kissing him back.

"It's not that bad." Wolf lifted his black hat off his head and settled it back in place. "I've had every extra man here scouting. Over a hundred of them returned to the Buffalo Commons on their own."

Wyatt jerked his head up and said sharply, "I sent Anna and the boys over there. Are they all right?"

"I've been in contact with them. Anna, Cody, and Colt, as well as Sally and Jeanie, are at the Commons, all sleeping like babies. Anna got the boys to bed and told me she was heading there herself."

"So only 121 buffalo loose," Wyatt sneered.

"Look"—Buffy turned on him—"I've about had it with—"

"I said we found *over* a hundred." Wolf talked over her, which was a good idea.

She clamped her mouth shut.

Wolf went on. "We got an exact count on the ones we loaded in the semis, so we're sure about them. Seth's taken the best head count back at the Commons, and he thinks there're more like 150. They're milling around, and we aren't firm on the number yet as a few more have wandered back in since they first found them. We've driven the ones there well away from the hole in the fence, but we've left the fence open, hoping more will come home."

"So only, say, seventy-five buff rampaging through my ranch. Great!" Wyatt was still holding his gun.

"Hey!" Buffy snatched the rifle out of his hand and stormed over to her rig and put it on the seat. "I'm sick of you stalking around with that dumb thing. You'd think you needed it to prove your manhood."

"Buffy, you're tired," Wolf said. "Don't start in on Wyatt."

Buffy waved her hand at Wolf. "I can't stand here and listen to him whine for another second!"

"Whine?" Wyatt wheeled on her.

She tilted her head up, way up, so she could meet his eyes. "If I have to listen to one more smart remark from you, I won't be responsible for my actions."

Wyatt sneered. "Not responsible. I'd say that about sums it up."

She realized she could see him. The sun was coming up. Wyatt was exhausted. She was exhausted. She knew he didn't deserve this, but her control was hanging by a thread. She tried to get away from him. "I've got buffalo to find." Buffy spun around on her heel.

Wyatt grabbed her arm, and she spun right back. He hauled her hard against his chest. "I've been working all night trying to clean up the mess you made." He shook her arm.

She jerked against his grip, and when he didn't let go, it felt like the top of her head caught fire. "You get your hands off me, or I'll—"

Wolf shoved in between them. "I didn't finish. There aren't

seventy-five buffalo running loose, because quite a few calves got scattered. I've got men combing the area bringing them in. We've found twenty-three so far, and we've just started hunting."

"Th–there's one dead at Wyatt's place." Buffy forgot about Wyatt's grip for a second and felt tears sting her eyes. She had about fifty good reasons to cry, all of them still on the loose. Oh, who was she kidding? She had about 1,462 reasons. She looked at Wyatt's furious, exhausted face. 1,463.

"What now?" Wyatt yanked the brim of his hat low over his eyes. "Do I have to stand here while the poor little lady cries her eyes out? That's all I need!"

"It's getting light." Wolf pushed his hands out flat against their chests, and Wyatt let go of her arm.

Buffy had to step away from Wyatt or start fighting with Wolf.

"We don't have time for this. Let's get to work rounding up the rest of those buff." Wolf said to Wyatt, "I've got a half dozen tranquilizer guns in the back of my truck. I'll hand them out. We'll post guards around your cattle and every other herd around. We'll stay connected by the CBs."

"How many men do you think you have?" Wyatt asked cynically.

Buffy wondered herself. Wolf sure was promising a lot of manpower.

"I've got all I need. Mr. Leonard's Learjet is expected in with twenty men on board. They're all off-duty forest rangers he contacted in and around Yellowstone, so they're top men. They're used to working with buffalo. He's rounding up another twenty out of Wyoming. And he's coming out personally to make sure this whole thing turns out right. Having the Buffalo Commons succeed is important to him, and this is a major screw-up. He's going to take whatever steps are necessary to make sure it never happens again. We'll get them, Wyatt. By the time we finish counting the dead, we might find out we've got all of them already."

"Yeah, I'll bet," Wyatt said bitterly.

Buffy reached past Wolf to throttle Wyatt.

Wolf caught her hand. He said to Wyatt, "Grab a tranquilizer gun."

"For her?" Wyatt asked icily.

Wolf ignored him. "There aren't that many buff left to round up. Let's quit talking and start looking. You take Buffy's truck, and we'll head back to the Commons."

Wolf boosted Buffy into his truck before she knew what happened. She wanted to go with Wyatt. She had a few more things she wanted to say to him.

Wyatt tore out of the yard, leaving a trail of dust a mile high.

❧

"Leonard looks like he's on top of the world," Buffy observed sourly as Leonard came out of the house to meet them. She hadn't been thinking clearly enough to send a truck out to the landing strip, but Wolf must have remembered.

"He loves it out here." Wolf pulled his truck to a stop and tugged a handkerchief out of his pocket, wiping dirt and sweat off his forehead. "The other times he's visited, he's always been excited like this. Of course, I get the idea he's running on a pretty high voltage all the time. And he knows about the stampede; I had one of the men stay on the phone in contact with his jet."

"He's going to start writing checks, I suppose. I don't like to think of what Wyatt might have to say about that." She almost hoped Mr. Leonard would just leave it to her to handle. Wyatt might insult Mr. Leonard so badly that she'd end up fired. She thought glumly that she deserved whatever happened.

Leonard came striding toward the truck as Buffy and Wolf

climbed out. He extended his hand to Wolf and didn't so much as look sideways at her. Buffy felt energy coming off Mr. Leonard in waves. High voltage didn't do him justice.

She had never met him before now. She'd been hired for this job by his Buffalo Commons Department, or whatever Leonard called it. She'd received a congratulatory phone call from him once she'd accepted the job, but that was all. She'd heard he visited occasionally, not overnight and never with any warning.

"Wolf, it looks like you're getting things under control."

Wolf took a quick glance at Buffy, and she knew he expected her support in anything he said. "The buff are almost all rounded up, but there's been a lot of damage. They ran through our nearest neighbor's ranch yard. They destroyed two vehicles. A barn burned down. He's got some dead livestock, and his house is about half ruined. It's a mess, and it might be worse than that. His herd, if the buffalo get out with them—"

Mr. Leonard held up his hand, and Wolf fell silent. Buffy could tell Wolf didn't like it.

"I've got someone over there right now assessing the damage and making plans to set things right." Leonard talked like a machine gun, spraying his opinion at the world. "I've already talked with Shaw's niece. She's a very angry young lady. Apparently her car was in the line of the stampede. And I'm aware of the repercussions of my buffalo getting at his cattle. I hear you sent men to ride herd on all the cattle in the area to watch for buffalo trying to join the group. Good thinking, Wolf."

Buffy didn't bother to mention that she and Wolf had decided that together.

"I've got more men coming in. I've got aerial surveillance already underway. I've hired every local crop duster I could find, and they're being organized to fly a pattern over the whole area looking for buffalo. I've got a team of security experts coming in to make changes on the fence. I also want to put a dozen additional riders on the perimeter permanently. That's a dozen all the time, three shifts a day. I'd like to hire locals if you can find them. It pumps money into the local economy. In the meantime, I'm bringing in riders from outside. I'm committing an additional million dollars a year in salaries. Plus the expense for the fence. I want that fence to stand up to lightning or a tornado.

"That all sounds good, Mr. Leonard"—Buffy decided it was time to at least make herself heard—"but there's more than just money at stake. Mr. Shaw's children could have been killed. He's determined to get these buffalo out of here. If you'd talk to him, explain your commitment to endangered species, I think it would—"

"I've got business demanding my attention." Leonard looked at her for the first time, but he never quite made eye contact. He wrinkled his nose a little as if she smelled. He directed his comment to Wolf. "Flying out here from New York this morning wasn't part of my schedule. You'll have to handle community relations. When my assessors are done, they'll write Mr. Shaw a check. I'm going to add a quarter of a million dollars for emotional distress. That ought to take care of it. If he wants more than that, I'll hire an arbitrator to hammer out the details."

Buffy said, "It's not the money, Mr. Leonard. Wyatt's children were—"

When he waved his hand this time, Buffy almost jumped him.

Wolf settled his hand on her shoulder.

Still talking to Wolf, Leonard said, "I've got an associate who will be here tomorrow to begin restitution proceedings. Please relay any further damages to him." Leonard turned from them and began striding toward the Jeep that would drive him back to his flashy little jet.

He was walking so fast Buffy had to run to catch up with him. She wanted to grab his arm, but she was a little too intimidated to do it, which made her mad. "You can't just issue orders and walk away from this."

A uniformed pilot jumped to attention and came around to hold open the door to the Jeep.

Mr. Leonard turned for the first time and really looked. "You're Miss Lange, aren't you? You're supposedly in charge here?"

"That's right."

"I wouldn't have agreed to hire someone so young to fill in until the director I want was available if not for that 'Doctor' in front of your name and such impeccable references. I was led to believe you were a woman who could handle buffalo."

"I can handle them."

Mr. Leonard's lips curled in what could only be distaste.

She was filthy—she'd spent the night in a cloud of buffalo-churned dust—and she reeked. She'd earned this stink through brutal hours of hard work. Her hair was a rat's nest, and she hadn't even unpacked her makeup yet, if she had any Jeanie hadn't swiped. She had no wish to pass some sleazy test of beauty administered by Mr. Leonard, but still his disgust stung.

"I'll make any unhappy people happy, and you will do your job and keep your mouth shut. Refer any reporters to my public relations division. They're preparing to handle everything. If any quotes in the press come from you, you'll lose this job, and the people who work with buffalo are few and far between, Miss Lange. I'm a major supporter of most of the work that is being done with them in both the public and private sector. The wrong word from me could make you a pariah."

The pilot, deaf by all appearances, waited until Mr. Leonard finished threatening her and got in. The pilot slammed the door, climbed behind the wheel, and drove off.

"Santa Claus in a Learjet," Wolf said sarcastically, coming up beside her while they watched the Jeep disappear over the rise to the runway. "Ho, ho, ho."

"Did you hear what he said?" Buffy was still gasping from the shock.

"Every word. That's the way he operates. He didn't get to where he is by being a soft touch."

"No, he got there by being a ruthless dictator."

Wolf tipped his head in agreement. "All he lacks is a country of his own and some weapons of mass destruction."

"Right now, Wyatt might think the buffalo counted as weapons." Buffy turned her thoughts from what could easily become the wreckage of her career. "I was sure Mr. Leonard would at least apologize to Wyatt in person. Although I have to admit, I was worried Wyatt might deck him. Now that I've met the man, I'm even more sure that's how it would have ended up."

"Oh, I don't know. He was pretty decent to me." Wolf's voice was droll, and the look he gave her told her he was waiting for her to explode.

She decided not to keep him waiting. "Who does that man think he is?" Buffy heard the jet fire up and watched to see if the noise made her herd stampede again. They ignored the noise. Then the plane disappeared into the sky. "I heard so much about community relations. And I thought this was more than a rich man's hobby. He's supposed to be a naturalist. How can he not stay and see if we get the buffalo rounded up? What about the environmental impact of this stampede? We could have damaged the ecosystem, destroyed wetlands, trampled nesting areas along the Cold Creek. . . . What can Leonard be thinking?"

"A more interesting question," Wolf said thoughtfully, "is why did he bother to come if he was only going to make a token appearance?"

"PR," Buffy said coldly. "If this leaks, the press will know he came. Mr. Sincerely Sorry inspecting the damage."

"Who in the press are we supposed to tell?"

Buffy said grimly, "Who indeed."

Wolf gave her a worried glance. "Buffy, you wouldn't."

"Actually no, I wouldn't. All we need is a bunch of reporters hanging around here."

"But you're tempted," Wolf said mildly.

"I'm tempted to do a lot of things I won't do. For example, I was tempted to knock Leonard on his backside for the way he talked to me. I didn't."

"Good girl. I was tempted to knock him down for the way he treated you."

Buffy jerked her gloves off her hands and tucked them behind her belt buckle. "Noticed that, did you?"

"Hard not to." Wolf rested his hand on her shoulder.

With Wolf's rugged support, Buffy allowed herself to feel the sting of Leonard's disrespect. It helped that Wolf had seen it and cared. "Let's go see how the head count is going."

seven

Wyatt sent the truck racing backward in time.

It was as if history were erasing itself as he barreled over the rough pastureland toward the hulking buffalo in the middle of his cattle. He was driving Buffy's own truck, near as he could tell. It had Oklahoma plates and her name on the registration. And Wyatt hadn't seen Wolf consult Buffy, so Wolf had probably not been in the right to lend it out, but Wyatt kept it anyway.

He raced his truck toward the buffalo and wished he had Gumby. He hadn't even been back to his place. He didn't know if Gumby or any of the rest of his horses were alive or dead. He didn't have time to go check, and besides, he couldn't stand to. Wolf had promised to send someone by and to take care of any injured animals. Wyatt had to see to his cattle.

He'd talked to Anna and the boys on the CB radio. Anna was still furious, but they were safe. He stuck his head out of Buffy's window and yelled, "Git out! Hyah!" He aimed the rig straight for the buff, and the big animal only raised its shaggy head and stared. Wyatt quit acting like a madman and stopped the truck so the buff was out the driver's side window about twenty feet away. He lifted the tranquilizer gun off the rack in the back window, took careful aim, and fired. The buffalo barely flinched, and that was more from the noise than the bright red dart stabbing into his flank.

While Wyatt waited for the sedative to take effect, he radioed Wolf. "It's a bull, and it's had plenty of time to breed with my cows."

"We'll be over with a stock trailer in fifteen minutes. We'll have him quarantined and checked for brucellosis and any other contagious diseases that could affect your cattle. If he's healthy, the worst that'll happen is a few of your cows'll have a calf that's half buff. This is the first one you've seen?"

"Yep. How's the head count?" Wyatt watched the buffalo waver and go down on one front knee and then the other.

"We've got twenty-five still missing. Now with the one you've got, it's twenty-four. We're hoping a few more will wander back to the Commons."

"Twenty-four buffalo running loose? We could be finding them for a long time."

"No, we're not letting up until we've got them all."

"Check along the creek. Grass is good. Lots of water. And there's tree cover, so they might be overlooked."

"I've already sent men on horseback along the river."

Wyatt sighed as he saw the buffalo's back end collapse. He lay with his head up, panting. "He's down. Are men on the way?"

"I'm halfway there already, Wyatt," Seth broke in on the CB. "Is there any damage to the school?"

"None I can see. What if this had happened a month later and the kids had been in school?"

Wolf broke in. "Don't go borrowing trouble."

"Yeah, I remember. I'm a whiner," Wyatt said acidly.

"I'm signing off." Wolf was gone with a *click*.

"I'm going to keep hunting, Seth. I've got five more pastures to check. You got enough men with you to load him?"

"We've come prepared. We appreciate the help."

"I'm not doing it to help you." Wyatt shut the CB off with a sharp *snap*. Seth didn't deserve to be barked at, but Wyatt didn't call him back. Instead, he drove toward his next pasture. He ran nearly forty thousand head of cattle on sixty thousand acres. He'd checked about half of them so far.

He found men stationed at the next two places. The men reported no sight of any buffalo. Midafternoon he found a year-old buff, injured but alive, hobbling alone miles from anywhere. After some concern with the dosage, Wyatt decided not to dart it. He called Wolf and stood guard on the calf until Seth showed up.

"Ten more have come home, and we found a small herd of them, eight in all, along the creek." Seth climbed out of his truck, his blond hair matted with dirt and sweat, exhaustion cutting lines in his face. "We should have them back on the Commons by nightfall. With this calf, we're down to four missing buff."

Wyatt sighed. "I've got one more pasture to check."

Seth reached behind the seat of his truck and dragged out a brown paper sack. "Got a sandwich and some coffee for you. Buffy packed it, said you probably hadn't eaten all day."

He hadn't. He took the sack gratefully.

The two men with Seth climbed out and started loading the calf. The calf was young and only had three good legs, but it was still a thousand-pound buffalo. He tried to kill them. They threw a lasso on him and held him cross-tied, but he didn't quit fighting.

Wyatt watched the two wrestle with the feisty little critter but didn't offer to help. He lifted his ancient black Stetson off his head and set it on the seat beside him while he ate the huge sandwich Buffy had sent out.

Egg salad. No meat, of course. But he was starving so he didn't complain. He'd save that for later when Buffy was handy.

He took a long drink of the hot coffee and let the caffeine ease into his blood. It was a brutally hot day, and Wyatt had been driving with the window open rather than running the air conditioner, afraid Buffy's engine might overheat.

"Thanks, Seth. The coffee helps." He felt the sweat beading

on his forehead from the hot liquid, and his already-soaked shirt was dripping. A light breeze wafted over him, and his wet shirt turned cold.

"You look beat, Wyatt. Time to call it a day."

"It's early yet." Wyatt drank deeply again and started a second sandwich.

"Seven o'clock."

"That's early."

"I know, but not when you were up all night. You're all in. We'll finish checking the herd. Leonard arranged a cleaning crew for your house and boarded up the windows. He's got the electricity back on and your phones working. So you've got a home to go to."

Wyatt felt a little lift from the day's brutal tension. He'd wondered where he'd sleep. "I've got six hundred head of unbred heifers with my best bull. They're the last herd I've got left to check. Has anyone been by the Johannsons'? Emily and her little sister are there alone these days."

"We've been up there several times. No sign of buffalo, but one might wander in. We've warned her to be on the lookout."

"I'll pull through there. My herd is right on the way."

"We can handle it. You need a break," Seth cajoled.

Wyatt got the distinct impression that the whole Buffalo Commons staff had been told to give him anything he wanted to head off a lawsuit. He had no intention of suing if Leonard made things right. But he didn't want them to quit worrying just yet.

"I'll stop in. And I don't need you riding out to my herd. My herd. My job."

Seth didn't argue anymore.

The two men with Seth strong-armed the wounded calf toward the cattle trailer.

For a moment, Wyatt and Seth watched the mayhem, and

Wyatt realized he was enjoying it. "They're beautiful critters in an ugly sort of way."

Seth nodded. "There's something, I don't know. . .majestic. . . about 'em. Working with 'em's the best job I've ever had. A'course they'd kill you soon as look at you, but I've learned my way around 'em, and it suits me. I'm sure sorry about the mess they made last night. I s'pose if you want it bad enough, you can shut us down over this."

"I'm not going to talk about that now. I'm still too mad to trust my own judgment."

The buffalo went in the trailer, a thousand-pound baby bawling for its mama. Seth drove off with a touch to the brim of his hat.

Wyatt headed for the last herd, the one farthest out. After he was sure they weren't being visited by the buffalo, he would go home, assess the damage to his place, then get Anna and the boys. He shouldn't have left them alone all day. He realized he'd trusted them to Buffy's care.

He didn't know why he'd trust a little woman who had done her best to ruin him, but he did. He didn't intend to think of almost kissing her either, but the mind is an unruly thing. She had been interested. Neither of them wanted it, but the night had worked its magic.

The truck drifted across the gravel road into the soft shoulder. The bouncing shook him awake, and he realized he was nearly asleep, lost in his daydream of Buffy's soft skin and gentle concern for him and his children.

And she'd known his boys apart.

He forced himself to quit thinking about how comfortable it had been to hold Buffy. Comfortable and dangerous.

The truck started bounding again. He got back on the road and turned his thoughts to his children. They'd been through a traumatic experience. Suddenly he was anxious to get done working and be a father.

He pulled onto the gravel road leading to the Johannsons'. The lights were blazing in Emily's house. A big beast of a buffalo cow was eating her front lawn.

Emily poked her head out the back door when Wyatt pulled up. He stayed in his truck. The animal was squarely between Wyatt's truck and the house. It didn't seem neighborly to sit in his truck and holler, but Wyatt had no intention of ending this awful day by having a buffalo do a Texas two-step on his face.

He contacted the Commons with his CB, and they advised him to dart the animal. Yeah, great advice. He'd have tried to hook her up to a halter and lead her home otherwise.

"Get back in the house, Em. I'm gonna put this big girl to sleep."

Emily and Stephie went inside to be well clear of the shooting. The buffalo looked at its flank, sniffed at the dart, and went back to munching.

The Johannson girls came back out.

"You okay in there?"

Emily nodded. "I'd already phoned. The Commons is sending a trailer to pick her up. How weird is this, a buffalo in my yard?"

Stephanie, Emily's little sister, smiled out at Wyatt and waggled her fingers in a wave. The two were a matched set. Long, straight brown hair and million-dollar smiles. They'd been living all the way out here alone since their father died. Emily had been adamant that Stephie not be uprooted. She'd given up college to be a lady rancher. The only one Wyatt had ever heard tell of.

"Are you all right? Any damage? Were you outside when it came up?"

"We've been hiding inside all day like a couple of houseplants. The hands from the Commons even did my chores for me."

"How's your herd?"

Emily shook her head. "Okay, I hope. It's a cow, so I don't have to worry about it too much."

"Did the twins get to see the buffalo?" Stephie asked. She went to the same school as his boys, and the Johannsons attended the same church as the Shaws.

They weren't close friends. Their ranches weren't far apart; the Johannson place was across a rugged stretch of land, and it wasn't often Wyatt came back this far.

The placid cow kept standing, so Wyatt stayed in the truck.

Emily asked about his place, and they chatted over the shaggy back of the buffalo until it dropped off to sleep. Emily invited him in.

"I've got one more herd to check before I'm done, so I'd better go."

A Commons truck pulled up with a trailer.

Wyatt had to wind around to get out of the hilly area surrounding the Johannsons'.

He came up on the herd and found a couple hundred young cattle surrounding the well nearest the road.

A man on horseback rode toward him.

"These are my cattle," Wyatt said. "Are you checking for buffalo?"

"Yep. Matt Grissom." The rider touched his hat politely. "Mr. Leonard had me fly in from his Wyoming ranch until we get the buffalo under control." The man had the same weathered, ageless look Wolf had. He wasn't an Indian, but his skin was deeply lined and baked to a deep brown; he also had the same wise, patient look in his eyes. Wyatt wondered if they got hired because of that look or if they started looking like that after they worked with buffalo for a while. "I haven't seen any sign of 'em out here, Mr. Shaw."

"It's Wyatt. Saves time."

The man nodded.

"I'm going to drive around. I've got a couple more wells on over the draw. This is only about a third of the herd."

The man sat up straighter. "I'm sorry. I thought this was the lot of 'em. I can ride out if you tell me which way."

"Nope, don't worry about it. I'd need to check 'em anyway."

"I'm going to radio in." The man jerked his thumb at a heavy-duty truck with a horse trailer on the back. He'd obviously driven himself and his horse out here. "I'm going to tell them we need more men to ride herd."

Wyatt waved and started driving.

Wyatt found another couple hundred head around the second well. He sighed with relief. He was one quick check away from quitting for the night. He wasn't doing a head count and knew that might be a mistake, but he was going to fall asleep at the wheel if he didn't get home. The cattle, especially young ones, tended to stay together. The one thing he had to make sure of was his bull. He hadn't been with any of the other heifers. He was about twice their size, and he stood off alone, often as not. He could be picked out at a glance.

Then he got to the next water hole, and it didn't even take a glance. He saw a bull dropping down off the back of a heifer—a buffalo bull. The buff moved on through the herd; then, at the sound of charging hooves behind him, the buff turned to face the enemy in the form of Wyatt's purebred Angus bull.

Wyatt watched as the two animals faced off, bellowing. Wyatt jammed his foot on the accelerator to get between them before his bull was killed. His bull had obviously been driven off once already, because there was an ugly gash the length of his belly.

The buffalo, a thousand pounds heavier and armed with slashing horns, raced toward Wyatt's ten-thousand-dollar bull. The Angus broke off the attack and ran. The buffalo charged after him until the Angus headed for the hinterlands. Then the buffalo turned toward his girls.

Wyatt had closed the gap between himself and the buffalo. He slammed on his brakes and drew the rifle. Taking careful aim, he darted the monster. The Angus disappeared over the hill.

Wyatt slammed his fist into the steering wheel and watched helplessly as his bull ran into some rugged land where his truck couldn't follow. He needed a horse.

He looked at the wavering buffalo and reached for the radio. Well, they'd told him he could have anything he wanted.

"This is Buffy. Come in."

"I've found another of your brutes. I've darted him, and he's going down. He was fighting my bull. My bull's hurt, cut up bad, and he's run off. I'm going to need a horse out here."

"We'll be out there as fast as we can travel."

Wyatt settled in as the sun began to lower in the sky. He'd only been sitting a couple of minutes before Buffy was on the horn again. "We're on the way. I'm bringing my vet bag so I can tend your bull."

"I would have considered darting my bull, but I was afraid the dosage in the tranquilizer gun was too high. We've only got a hour or so of daylight left. He was bleeding bad. If we don't find him before dark, we'll find him dead in the morning." Wyatt heard the exhaustion in his voice. His thoughts wouldn't move in a straight line anymore.

"Tell us exactly where you are, Wyatt."

Wyatt heard her talking as if she were fading away into the distance. "You've got a man out here. Matt. . .Matt something. Uh, he was watching my herd. He said he was going to call in for more help."

"Okay, we know where he is."

"I'm. . .I don't know. Near him."

"Wyatt, are you all right?" Buffy asked. "I'm not picking you up very well."

"That's a stupid question considering the day I've had," Wyatt said. "Of course I'm not all right." Then he wondered, without really caring, if he'd actually spoken out loud.

He tossed the CB mike in the general direction of the radio and leaned his head back on the headrest. He couldn't give Buffy any better directions. He was so tired he didn't know where he was.

eight

"There he is!"

Buffy aimed her truck at the herd of cattle surrounding the huge black lump on the ground.

Bill.

Their last escapee. Caught for the second time in two weeks by Wyatt Shaw. One angry cowboy.

"Why hasn't Wyatt answered the CB? Could he be hurt? I asked him if he was all right, and he said, 'Of course not.' What do you think he meant by that?"

"I don't know what he meant," Wolf said. "Same as I didn't know two minutes ago when you asked me and five minutes before that and four minutes before that and. . ."

Buffy leaned forward until her nose almost touched the windshield and talked over Wolf's recital of her nagging. "You know, I see his truck, but I don't see him. Do you see him in the truck? What if he's not in there? Where could he have gone?"

Wolf's only answer was a groan; Wolf had put in a long, hard day, and Buffy knew he wasn't inclined toward idle chatter at the best of times.

Buffy pulled up to the truck—her truck—and saw Wyatt slumped low in the seat behind the steering wheel. She jumped out of the rig before it had come to a full stop and raced to the door. "Wyatt! Wyatt, are you all right?"

He jumped so hard he cracked his head on the roof. "Ouch!"

Buffy noticed he didn't swear, which was something she was used to—being around men so much. But he put enough feeling in "ouch" to reassure anyone listening he was furious.

Buffy yanked open the truck door. "Are you all right?" She laid her hand on his scowling cheek, wondering that she didn't shrink away from his anger.

"Yes, I'm all right!" His tone nearly left bite marks. "I just caught a few minutes' sleep. Did you bring me a horse? I've got to ride out and check on my bull."

"Yes, we've got you a horse." Buffy knew she should be trying to appease Wyatt because of Mr. Leonard's worry about being sued, but all she could think of was helping him because she wanted to.

"*That* bull?" Wolf asked softly.

They all turned. Wyatt's black bull, with the ugly wound, vicious red against his shining ebony hide, stood panting on a sandy hilltop about a thousand yards away.

"That's him." Wyatt stepped out of the truck. "Wolf, what about the dosage?"

"We reduced the dosage in one of our tranquilizers." Wolf produced the altered medicine from his shirt pocket. "Cut it a little more than in half."

Buffy studied the big bull. Nowhere near as big as Bill, now sleeping peacefully, but the bull was still a huge animal. "It might not even knock him out, but it will make him docile. He looks pretty nervous up there."

They watched the bull stomp his forelegs and bob his head. Every once in a while, the prairie wind would catch the sound of a deep bellow and carry it to them.

Buffy caught back the words of apology. Surely somehow, someday, something could pass between her and Wyatt that didn't require "I'm sorry." No one had gotten around to apologizing for that almost kiss yet. Of course, they'd been interrupted. They might have gotten around to it.

"Better dart him," Wolf said. "He's ready to run right now."

"I'll treat him out here if it's not too serious. If he needs more, we'll load him and take him back to the ranch." She took the red-flagged dart from Wolf and handed it to Wyatt. "Wolf said you're the man to take the shot."

Wyatt took the dart. He loaded his rifle without taking his eyes off his bull. "I can't get him from here, not with this gun. I'll drive a little closer. If I can get my truck between him and the buffalo, he might even come in for me. On a normal day, he'd walk right up and put his head in my cab."

"Well, this will never qualify as a normal day. I'll drive." Buffy climbed behind the wheel of her truck, and Wyatt got in the passenger's side.

"I've got a horse in the trailer if we need him." Wolf jerked a thumb at the truck he and Buffy had come in. "And an empty trailer on the way. I'll get things ready to load Bill when he wakes up."

Wyatt gave the sleeping buffalo a startled look. "That's Bill?"

"Yeah, your old buddy," Buffy said.

"Will it hurt him to be sedated again so soon?"

Buffy was amazed when he sounded like he cared. "It shouldn't. Did you check and see if he was breathing?"

Wyatt gave her a sideways glance. "I took a nap."

"Look, your bull is coming in." Buffy tipped her head.

"Pull the truck forward until the bull can't see Bill." Wyatt carefully settled the rifle between them, muzzle pointed down.

Once Buffy had the truck in place, the Angus eased his way down the hill. He seemed to be at full strength, although he made skittish movements.

"He's usually so calm," Wyatt said. "A lazy old lug."

Buffy watched the bull prance forward.

"Do you toss hay out of your truck the way Wolf does for the buffalo?"

"Yeah, so they come when they hear the truck motor." Wyatt stepped out of the truck so he had a clear range of fire. "We could bulldog him, but I think it's better if he's asleep."

"Good. I can sew up his side and check for any muscle damage. If we aren't satisfied with how he responds, we can take him in."

Wyatt raised the gun and took aim. His hands were steady as steel on the rifle. He lowered it. "You're sure this stuff won't hurt him?"

"We use it a lot with the buffalo. I learned the prescribed dose for cattle in vet school. I'm sure."

Wyatt aimed. The bull walked straight toward them, and Wyatt shot him.

The bull jumped and looked at Wyatt accusingly.

"I know how you feel, old boy." Wyatt hung the rifle up on the gun rack Buffy had in her truck. "Betrayed."

Wyatt didn't look at Buffy, but she got the message. A motor drew her attention. Another stock trailer pulled up.

Wolf trailed after the truck on foot. He looked over. "They're here for Bill."

Wyatt turned back to his bull without comment. His eyes were bloodshot. He was still a young man, but the sun and wind had already begun weathering lines around his eyes. Those lines were deeper than they had been yesterday, and Buffy blamed herself for that.

He ran his forearm across his brow and lifted his black Stetson with one hand to shove some unruly dark hair off his face with the other. He replaced the hat to anchor his sweat-soaked hair.

She had to try. One more apology. Maybe she'd stop screwing up after this. "Wyatt, I'm sorry."

"I know," he said shortly.

"The words don't mean anything, and Mr. Leonard's money only goes so far."

"You know how long I planned for that bull there?"

Wolf split a look between them and went back to the buffalo.

Buffy wished he'd stay and let Wyatt divide his anger, which made her a coward on top of everything else. "I know a purebred bull is an extremely valuable animal. You've got a herd that's pure black. The Angus breed is especially valuable. He's worth a lot of money."

"Ten years." Wyatt stared at the bull whose head was now hanging low. The bull's legs wobbled. "My dad and I decided we were going to get away from the more exotic breeds. We had white Charolais mainly. I've got Simmental and Chianina mixed in. Those are big breeds. For a long time, it was the theory that you'd buy the smallest cow around—that's Angus or Hereford—and breed them to the biggest bull. The cow is cheap to feed because she's little, and the calf will grow fast and give you a better return, but we started having trouble calving."

"Those little cows giving birth to whopping big calves." Buffy nodded. "I was called in during my last year of college to do a lot of cesareans."

"Which costs a lot and is risky for the cow, and there goes your profit. So Dad and I started going back to straight Angus, but we wanted to do it right. There was so much mixed blood in the breed that we weren't sure what we were getting. We decided to get a purebred. A purebred Angus has really beautiful lines. They're a healthy, hardy animal that thrives in the conditions in the Black Hills. We probably didn't need to get one as expensive as that one."

Wyatt's bull wavered. He was standing about thirty feet in front of them. When he staggered sideways, Buffy got a better look at the ugly slash in his side. Blood dripped from his belly and ran down his legs. This close, Buffy could see smaller cuts on the bull's head and neck, and one leg was badly lacerated. It was obscene on the proud, beautiful animal. The bull dropped to one front knee. Buffy prayed that he hadn't lost so much blood the dosage she used would kill him. She told Wyatt nothing would go wrong, but the world played cruel tricks, or at least that had been her experience. She could have prayed all night and not covered everything that could go wrong.

"He was worth it," Buffy said as the bull dropped another knee. "He's magnificent."

"Dad was finally going to retire and have a little fun. He surprised me with the bull on the day I bought the ranch. Dad sold for a fraction of what he could have gotten from Mr. Leonard, but Dad had lived like a miser and saved a lot of money; he didn't need Leonard's cash. And his father had handed it on to him for a token payment, so he wanted to do that for me. Still, not every rancher in the area made the same decision for their sons. A lot of my friends who had hopes of ranching left when their fathers couldn't afford to pass up Leonard's money."

Buffy opened her mouth to give her usual automatic support for Mr. Leonard the naturalist, but she couldn't speak the words, not after his ruthless performance this morning. She no longer believed Leonard's motives were so pure.

"I could have paid market value for the land, because Jessica had just died and I got a life insurance payment." Wyatt pursued the subject of his wife. "But instead, here I am buying the place for a song, and Dad comes up with Coyote there as a present."

"Coyote? You named him?" The bull's back end sagged to the prairie grass, and Buffy reached into her truck and picked up her vet bag.

"Not really. He's got one of those million-dollar names, Marquis Blazing Star Stewart. I think that's it. I just call him 'the bull.'" Wyatt got out, and the two of them walked toward the dazed bull. "But sometimes we call him Coyote after USD."

"After what?"

Wyatt gave her a look that was pure disgust. "The football team?"

"Your local high school?" Buffy thought that might be a normal conversation they could have. She'd gone to high school. . .for a while. She'd graduated early, and she'd taken college classes the whole time and spent every summer and holiday and weekend working with buffalo, so she hadn't socialized much. But she'd been to an occasional football game. Never cared for them, but still. . .

Wyatt snorted. "The University of South Dakota. It's where I met Jessica." He got near enough to touch the bull and carefully knelt beside him. He patted the bull's stout shoulder. "Sorry about this, old man. Bet you never figured on having to fight a monster like that for the girls, did you?"

Buffy ran her hands over the bull. The worst wound, the one in his side, had hanging flaps of skin. She'd be sewing all night. The bull panted steadily, and she breathed a sigh of relief. His neat, black head drooped like it weighed a ton.

"Let's see if we can roll him onto his side."

The bull went down flat without a protest. His feet flayed around a bit, but there was no strength behind them.

Wolf came trudging across the prairie carrying a cardboard box. "Bill's starting to wake up. We're ready to load him. This is everything you brought to tend the bull."

"Thanks, Wolf. Just set it here beside me."

Wolf laid the box down then knelt beside the bull so he, Buffy, and Wyatt were lined up down the length of his belly, Wolf nearest his head. "He's a fine animal, Wyatt. He's young and strong. He'll be okay."

"Yep, I think he'll make it."

"You could go back with Wolf, Wyatt. I'll be at this for a long time, and it's really a one-woman job." Buffy glanced at the setting sun. It had to be nearly nine o'clock at night. Would this day never end?

"I'll stay."

"I have the CB if I need any help. You look exhausted."

"I'll stay."

Buffy had known he would. The truth was she didn't want to be left alone out here. But she'd had to try. "Fine."

Wolf gave the bull an affectionate slap on the neck, and the bull started. It blinked its eye resentfully at Wolf as if it didn't want its sleep disturbed.

"Don't like lettin' anyone else be in charge, do you, boy?" Wolf got up with a grunt of exertion that told Buffy how tired he was. He walked back to the buffalo.

Buffy immediately began rummaging in her box.

"Tell me what to do, Buffalo Gal."

"I already told you it was a one-woman job."

"I can sew up torn skin as well as you most likely. We can be out of here in half the time."

Buffy pulled battery-operated hair clippers out of the box Wolf had brought. "I want to clip the area along the wound; then I'll disinfect and wash it. Then I'm going to pack it with antibiotic powder, and I'll start sewing."

"Let's get on with it."

Buffy gave Wyatt a long look. She saw his determination and gave up on working alone. She didn't like kneeling here beside him, shoulder to shoulder, his warmth seeping into her, his scent teasing her on the soft evening breeze. She clicked the clippers, and they came on with a tooth-tingling buzz.

The noise prevented them from talking, which was just as well. Between exhaustion and anger, she didn't think Wyatt had anything to say she wanted to hear. But the bull didn't need to be shaved bald. The skin along the big wound and several small ones was clear in a few minutes. While Buffy worked in the bloody fur, cleaning the wound, Wyatt cleaned beside her. She heard Wolf drive away, leaving her and Wyatt alone with Wyatt's herd and the big bull sleeping under their hands.

She'd just gotten comfortable with the silence when Wyatt said, "He bred at least one of my heifers. I wasn't quick enough to see which one. The buff calf'll kill her. My Angus are too small to give birth to a baby buffalo. Look at this wound on his back leg." Wyatt pointed to a cut with the blood dried to a hard black crust. "He got this cut hours ago. That buffalo has been out here all day. Who knows how many he bred."

Buffy examined the muscle wall under the cut for damage. "Bill hadn't really been accepted into the herd yet. While the rest of them ran together, he just wandered a different way. And this pasture isn't that far from the Commons as the crow flies. Yes, I'd say we need to figure he's been with this herd most of last night and all day today."

Wyatt never quit working. "All these heifers are the age to be bred. I could lose a dozen of them, and if Bill is carrying brucellosis or any other disease, the state has to quarantine at least this whole herd until they're tested and found healthy. If even a few of them are sick, I could lose six hundred head of my best young stuff."

Buffy shook her head. "Bill is healthy. He was checked carefully before we moved him here."

"And he's been with your herd for two weeks or so, right? Are you sure every buffalo cow you've got is healthy? Are you sure none of them has passed anything on?"

"No, that's possible, but not likely. Look, I'm sorry—"

"Stop! Stop with 'I'm sorry!'" Wyatt roared. Then he clamped his mouth shut.

In the deepening dusk, Buffy saw his determination to control his temper and the exhaustion that weakened his iron will. She was just as tired. She almost reached for him, but she knew that was exactly the wrong thing to do. She knew buffalo men, and Wyatt was cut from the same cloth. The refining fires of the West forged them into pure, unalloyed steel. She had a desire to comfort him that was purely female. She recognized it as a better part of herself. But she was also a woman who'd worked with mean animals and hard men all her life. She squelched her softer instincts.

"All right, forget sorry. Forget Leonard will make it right. Forget all of that. Just get over it."

Wyatt's eyes, drooping with exhaustion, popped open. "Get over it?"

"That's right, you heard me." She faced him. "Get over it! It happened. You'll do whatever you need to do to get through today, and then you'll get through tomorrow. That's life. This is an ugly mess, and it may get uglier, and you'll do whatever you have to do. Anything else you say about it is just *whining*!"

Wyatt's jaw tightened until she thought his teeth might crack. He glared at her with those blazing hazel eyes. It wasn't the first time he'd burned her with them. It wasn't the first time she'd accused him of whining. She almost smiled.

Wyatt was the strongest man she'd ever met, and she'd met some strong ones. If ever a man had a right to complain, it was Wyatt Shaw.

He breathed in and out. His nostrils flared, his eyes got hotter, and he rose to her challenge. "That's right. I'll do whatever tomorrow brings, because the sun will rise tomorrow, and I don't have any choice but to live through it."

Buffy was so proud of him she wanted to. . . Well, never mind what she wanted to do—it was a bad idea. "So you stay here"— she jabbed a crimson finger at the bull's belly—"and you survive as best you can, and I will, too. So I'm sorry—not because it's my fault—it isn't! I'm sorry because I know your life is going to be a complicated mess for a while. And then it will be over."

"My life?" Wyatt asked.

"No, this mess!"

"And what?" Wyatt sneered. "We'll all look back on this and laugh?"

"I don't see much chance of that."

Their gaze held a moment; then she went back to sterilizing the cuts. Out of the corner of her eye, she saw Wyatt's fist clench for a second; then he turned to his bull and began working alongside her again. It was almost companionable—in a demilitarized zone kind of way.

Buffy sprinkled topical antibiotic on the wounds. "The bleeding has stopped. He would have been okay without our help if he could have avoided an infection. The skin flap might have caught on something and gotten worse, and it would have left him with an ugly scar."

"Well, we wouldn't want him to be ugly, now, would we?" Wyatt said dryly.

Buffy threaded a needle and handed it to Wyatt then got one for herself. The big bull breathed in and out but was otherwise still.

"I don't see muscle damage." The bull's eyes fluttered open once in a while. "He's not really unconscious. He's just stoned out of his gourd."

Wyatt laughed as he sewed. "What is that stitch you're using?"

"It's a little more difficult than the one you're doing. I'm not that long out of vet school, so maybe it's something new."

Buffy showed Wyatt how to do it, and he adapted to her method. "I'll bet this would leave less of a scar."

"Oh, not really. Your stitch isn't going to leave a scar that'll show once his hair grows back."

"I meant on myself."

Buffy's hands dropped to her sides. "You mean you sew your own cuts?"

"Yeah, sure."

Buffy grimaced. She thought of scarring and pain and infection, and finally all she could say was, "That'd hurt."

"It hurts some, but usually you're already hurting like crazy, what with having a cut big enough it needs to be stitched. A few more pinpricks don't make much difference, and I'm a long way from a doctor out here."

"You've really done it?" Buffy was having a hard time imagining a man taking a needle to his own flesh.

Wyatt paused to unsnap his sleeve and shove it up to his elbow. A jagged cut ran the length of his left arm. "I did this one. If it'd been on my right arm, I might have needed to go in."

Buffy didn't like the looks of the nasty scar. "A doctor could have done better for you. You wouldn't have that scar."

Wyatt gave a rusty half laugh. "Yeah, I'm ruined. My dreams of being Miss America are over." He reached for the thread.

"Do you sew the boys up?"

"Of course. With those two wild animals, I'd be running to the doctor for stitches twice a week. I just sewed a cut on Cody's foot a few days ago. I wouldn't do it if I thought he was hurt seriously. I'd want a doctor to rule out any complications. But he kicked his bare foot through a window and slit the top of his arch."

"And he lay still for it?"

"No," Wyatt said, as if she'd lost her mind. "That kid has never laid still, night or day, in his life."

"How'd you get him sewn up?"

"I wrapped him up so tight in a bedsheet he wasn't able to move a muscle. The doctor taught me that years ago."

"You're saying a doctor knew about this and didn't demand you bring him in?"

"Who do you think taught me to put stitches in? Well, I mean besides my mom. A doctor gave me some good tips that improved my methods. The first time I did it, Cody was two years old. I wrapped him up, and Jessica held him down. He screamed the whole time, and I bet anything I've got hearing damage from it. And Colt thought we were killing him, so he screamed, too. It wasn't pretty."

"How could you stand it?"

Wyatt shrugged. "It would have been stupid to drive fifty miles to a doctor and make that poor guy listen to the screaming. And I'd have had to listen to it, too, in the doctor's office. It was our problem. We took care of it."

Buffy didn't want to ask about Wyatt's wife, but her mouth took charge. "Your wife must have been tough."

"No, actually she hated me for it the first time I did it in front of her." Wyatt laughed, and Buffy heard affection in his laugh. "Cody had cracked his chin and needed a couple of stitches. My wife cried the whole time, but she held him down for me. Then she fainted dead away when it was over, so I had an unconscious wife and two screaming kids on my hands. Long afternoon."

Wyatt sighed. "I had to call a neighbor lady to hold him when we took them out. He screamed just as loud, and it didn't hurt him a bit, and Jessica wouldn't speak to me for a week afterward."

Buffy put the last stitch in the bull's belly; then she turned to several lesser cuts on his head and neck. Wyatt began stitching on the back leg.

Buffy said, "She cried, but she did it. She sounds like a hardy woman."

"Jessica hated the ranch. She spent more time not speaking than she did speaking."

"But she stuck with you?" Buffy straightened and looked at Wyatt. "Even though it was a life she hated?"

Wyatt quit sewing and looked sideways at her. "Sure she stuck with me. We made a commitment to God and to each other.

We both intended it to last for a lifetime." He paused then added quietly, "She was never happy, though. I was born to be a rancher. Never wanted anything else. But the year I graduated from high school, Dad was talking about retiring. I was born when he was older, and it was just too much responsibility for me. I wasn't ready for my whole life to be laid out and settled. I went off to college, thinking I could leave these Black Hills behind. I met Jessica while I was there."

"She wasn't raised on a ranch?" Buffy asked.

"About as far from a ranch as you can get. She was from a suburb in Connecticut. Her dad commuted into New York City every day to work."

"How did she ever get to South Dakota?"

"Oh, it's a long story. Something about a friend whose grandmother had spent her childhood here and always loved the country. How does anyone end up anywhere?"

Buffy thought of all the twists and turns that had led her here.

"She fell in love with the idea of the wide-open spaces ringed by these rough mountains. I'm sure I was homesick and talking about missing the land. She got excited about getting back to nature; then she fell in love with me." Wyatt smiled fondly.

Buffy looked back at her patient to distract her from an uncomfortable pang of jealousy.

"By the end of the first semester at the university, I knew I'd be miserable anywhere but out here. I told her I was quitting school and going home to ranch, and I asked her to marry me. She said yes."

"After only dating for a few months?"

Wyatt shrugged. "We were just kids, still in that first glow of new love. It all seemed like a miracle. I got out just long enough to find the woman of my dreams. She came all the way across the country to be an earth mother. We were going to have six kids and eat food out of our garden, and she'd sew our clothes and knit our sweaters. We eloped and came home for Christmas to tell my folks we were married and ask if we could have my old room. My folks were thrilled. Jess was pregnant by New Year's. By the end of January, she was stir-crazy."

"This is a beautiful place to live, Wyatt. But it's not for everybody."

"She sure wasn't suited to it. She wanted more socializing, more regular hours. Her folks had a lot of money, and she was used to traveling and shopping in stylish stores."

Buffy looked down at her sweat-soaked cotton work shirt and bloody Levis. "Culture shock, huh?"

"Big-time. The weird part of it was, her classy clothes and her urban attitude were the things I was most attracted to. So I was asking her to give up what I loved most about her."

"She would have adjusted eventually. All she really needed was time."

"Time just made it worse. She didn't like worrying about snow and drought. It wore on her. She cried a lot and yelled even more. She didn't want to live with my folks, but there weren't any other livable houses around. I might have bought us a trailer, but there were days her mood was so black I didn't feel. . ." Wyatt fell silent.

Buffy turned to listen more closely.

He cleared his throat. "I didn't feel comfortable leaving the boys with her. I wasn't sure. . .I wasn't sure what she might do. So we stayed with my folks. And about two years ago, she died in car wreck." Wyatt's voice faded to a whisper. "I've often wondered when she died if it wasn't a relief for her."

"Was it that bad?"

Wyatt thought about it; then he turned back to his stitching, and Buffy thought he might refuse to answer. She started sewing again, too. They were nearly done. This horrible day might finally be drawing to a close.

The bull began moving restlessly as the sedative wore off.

"She never could tell the boys apart. Not even when they were older."

Buffy said incredulously, "They barely resemble each other. How could someone not tell them apart?"

Wyatt laughed. "Buffalo Gal, they look so much alike the teacher at their school makes me come in with them every morning and tell her which is which. They tried to trick her almost every day until we started doing that. It wouldn't have mattered much except the boys have a habit of fooling someone and then laughing like loons when they're done with their prank. It made the teacher mad to be lied to all the time, and it really made her mad to be laughed at."

"Haven't you had a talk with her? I mean, Cody's eyelashes are thicker, and Colt must outweigh him by quite a bit."

"Two pounds," Wyatt supplied.

Wyatt leaned away from the bull and groaned as his back cracked. "I know just what you mean, but the teacher doesn't see it. She suggested I put an *X* on the back of their necks in different colors of indelible ink so she could tell."

Buffy gasped. "She wanted to mark them? Like wild animals that have been darted and tagged by the Wildlife Service? That's awful!"

"Kinda struck me that way, too." Wyatt put the needle back in Buffy's satchel and reached for the thermos of hot water she'd brought. The bull stirred his legs, and Wyatt eased away from the big animal. Coyote lifted his head and moaned out a plaintive *moo* then let his head drop back to the ground.

"He's coming around. Give him some room." Wyatt poured warm water over first one hand and then the other. Buffy shifted her supplies out of the way of moving hooves, and Wyatt poured the water for her to wash. "In the teacher's defense, those two rascals were tormenting her. You know what they're capable of."

Buffy sniffed. "She sounds incompetent to me."

"Now, darlin', we don't go bad-mouthing teachers out here. We're still in that old-fashioned mode where if the teacher punishes you at school, you get punished again when you get home."

Buffy said aghast, "You really do that? You side with the teacher against your boys?"

"Every single stinkin' time, regardless of the circumstances. You've met my boys, right?"

"Even if they are active—"

Wyatt cut in, "And I've gone to church with Mrs. Rogers for forty years. She was my teacher back in the day. I'd trust her with my life, and I trust her with my boys. Besides, I'm still kinda scared of her."

Buffy looked at Wyatt and tried to imagine him scared of anybody. She began to laugh.

Wyatt grinned. "I'm serious. She's tough." Wyatt leaned very close to her and whispered, "And I'll tell you another reason I side with her, but it's a secret."

They knelt inches from each other. He was too close. He had mischief in his eyes, and she could smell the hard scent of sweat and cattle and the prairie breeze on him. The metallic scent of blood was primitive like her reaction to Wyatt.

She should have moved away but instead she leaned closer. "What secret?"

With sparkling eyes, he said, "My boys run around shooting each other all the time. Drives everybody who knows 'em *crazy*."

"Wyatt!" Buffy sat back on her heels and swatted at him.

He caught her hand before she could do any damage. "You don't have any of those tranquilizer darts in a forty-pound dose, do you? Like two of them, maybe? To be administered at Cody and Colt's bedtime."

"Wyatt Shaw, don't you dare talk about your boys that way!" She tugged at her hand, but he didn't let go.

His voice was husky, and she barely heard him say, "This is so stupid."

Then he kissed her.

nine

Wyatt lost the battle, and the war wasn't looking good.

He pulled Buffy closer. The box of veterinary supplies was between them, and he shoved it aside and pulled her onto his lap. The shifting around gave him time to think, and he broke off the sweetest kiss he'd ever had. And that was a sad thing for a man to say who'd been married. He lifted his head, and she chased after him. He almost howled at the moon, he wanted to kiss her again so bad. Instead, he dropped her off his lap. "I shouldn't have done that."

Buffy's eyes were fixed on his lips. "I'll say."

Wyatt got to his feet and walked away from her about ten feet. He ran his hands through his hair and knocked his hat off his head. He clumsily caught it then tossed it aside on the dewy grass. He was far enough away from her that he couldn't see her expression. So he took a chance and faced her. "We both know that shouldn't have happened."

Buffy didn't answer. Instead, she rolled onto her hands and knees, turned away from him, and began packing her satchel with unsteady movements.

"Well, say something!" The bull's legs jerked when Wyatt yelled. Wyatt strode over to Buffy and yanked her to her feet. He gripped her upper arms. "It was stupid!"

"Very stupid." Buffy wrenched against his grip, and Wyatt had to hold on tight to keep his hands on her.

"Let go!"

Wyatt would never have let go if she'd fought him physically, but her voice, cold and angry, jarred him out of whatever madness had made him get this close.

He let go.

She turned and walked around the bull and crouched behind him. She was fussing with his eyelids, and she ran her hand down his neck. She reached for her vet bag across the bull's back in a way that made it clear she wanted to keep the bull between her and Wyatt. She fished around in the bag for a little bottle of medicine and with deft movements gave Coyote a shot of antibiotic. "I don't want to leave him out here unconscious. Why don't you go get some rest?"

"I'm not leaving you. You don't even have a way back."

"There's someone riding herd nearby all night."

"I thought you said Bill was the last. Why would someone still be riding herd?"

"Because we're doing a final head count in the morning, and we aren't going to let up on your herd until we've double-checked. You'll go right past him. Tell him to bring his truck over this way later and check on me."

"Forget it. You go. I'll stay."

"I'm the vet. And I'm the one with the escaped buffalo. This is my responsibility."

"My ranch. My bull. My responsibility."

"Okay, then go away so you can keep yourself from doing something as stupid as kissing me again!"

Wyatt had to give her that one. He did need to get away from her. Because now he heard the hurt in her voice and his own insult coming from her mouth. He knew the best way to make it better was to pull her back into his arms and tell her it wasn't stupid, that it was the best idea he'd had in a long time. *Years. Ever.*

"Buffy, you know I'm a Christian."

Buffy didn't answer.

"I don't kiss women to entertain myself." He planted his

hands on his hips and felt the evening breeze ruffle his hair. He tried to drink in the cool of the night.

"Good, because that wasn't very entertaining." Coyote stirred, and Buffy got behind him and heaved when he tried to sit up.

Wyatt ignored that crack because he'd felt the way she responded to him. She'd been entertained almost out of her mind. Just like him. "So, I'm not going to kiss you again."

"Good. I agree. It's unanimous." Her voice could have taken bites out of his hide.

Wyatt knew the bull didn't really need her help, but she looked like she needed to keep busy. "And the opposite of kissing for entertainment is getting serious, and we both know it can't be anything serious, because you're headed for the job of your dreams, and I'll live out the rest of my life alone before I ask some woman to choose me over anything else."

"You're absolutely right: It can't be serious! Because I'd rather be an old maid than get involved with a man who thinks it's his right to dominate the whole world!" She yelled, but her hands were gentle as they ran over the bull's black coat.

Wyatt tried to remember Jessica ever touching any of his livestock like that. She wouldn't go near the cattle, not even the baby calves. She said they smelled bad. She was scared of the horses. Gathering eggs had been his job, too.

"So that's it. Nothing serious, nothing foolish. That leaves nothing."

"Nothing," Buffy agreed. She fell silent as she petted the big bull. Coyote shook his head and huffed a slobbery sneeze. Angus snot sprayed Buffy's neck and arm and the front of her bloody shirt. She wiped her neck negligently on one hunched shoulder with an *ugh* of disgust. Then she wiped her arms off on the bull's neck and slapped him affectionately on the shoulder. "Cut that out, you old coot."

She was filthy, and she smelled like a cow herd in July. She was soaked in blood, and she wanted Wyatt to stay away from her. But she kissed like a dream and knew his boys apart, and she didn't mind bull slobber.

Wyatt fell in love.

What jolted his body wasn't a timid feeling. It wasn't particularly joyful either, because it wasn't possible for them to be together. What it was, was real. It was a fully formed emotion that invaded him down to his cells and his chromosomes and definitely down to his heart. It was something that made what he'd felt for his wife pale and superficial. . .and heartbreaking.

Allison "Buffy" Lange was the most interesting, touchable, honest woman he'd ever known, coated with the hide and temperament of a buffalo. And he knew with an already-broken heart that he was going to love her for the rest of his life.

The bull flinched slightly when she slapped him and twisted his head to look over his shoulder at her.

"Sorry." Buffy patted more gently. "I know you've had a rough day. Why don't you get up for me, big boy? Show me some of that purebred heart."

As if he were listening to her, the bull lurched to its feet with a grunt. Buffy jumped to her feet and backed away, shouting encouragement. The bull stood, wavering a bit for a few seconds; then it began walking down toward the water tank that stood by the windmill. It walked out from between them, and Wyatt had to tense every muscle in his body to keep from closing the space.

He wanted to beg her to forget buffalo and all her years of education and come home and help him identify his boys. She'd only have to give up her life's work, her dreams, her future.

He estimated it would take about six weeks for her to start resenting him.

Buffy watched the bull walk away, and Wyatt used that time to get ahold of himself. He turned, his muscles resisting his mind, and started packing up her medical supplies.

She had done most of it already, and it was the work of seconds to finish. When he was done, he trusted his voice. "Let's go. It's probably too late for me to see the boys tonight, but I'd like to get some sleep."

Buffy turned from watching the bull, picked up the satchel while Wyatt grabbed the box, and started for the pickup. "You'd better come back to the Commons and sleep with me."

"What?" Wyatt nearly strangled on the word. Then he hurried to catch up with her.

"Your house is probably livable, with the cleaning crew and repairs we've done. The carpeting was ruined, by the way. Anna gave the go-ahead to replace it with the same color. She said it was the color of dirt and you'd never keep up with anything else. Anna and the boys will be at my place. We've got plenty of room for you in the bunkhouse."

Oh.

Wyatt waited for the blood to start flowing to his head. "Okay. I'm too tired to look at my place anyway."

They drove back to the Commons in a strained silence that Wyatt couldn't breach, because everything he had to say was a big mistake.

Buffy pointed to the bunkhouse.

"I know my way."

"I had my men bring you a change of clothes, which will be on the first empty bunk in the door. Shower and come up to the house. There'll be some supper for you."

Wyatt wasn't going anywhere near her house, especially not if she was clean and sweet-smelling. He was so hungry his stomach had started gnawing on his innards, but he wasn't going in. "I'll pass on the supper. I'm dead on my feet."

Buffy didn't look at him. "Okay, then." She agreed so easily that Wyatt was sure she wanted to get away from him. He wondered if it was for the same reason he wanted to get away from her. And perversely that made him want to stick like a buffalo burr.

As she walked away, she said over her shoulder, "Tomorrow we'll begin damage assessment on your ranch. And we'll decide what we're going to do about your heifers having a buff calf. How long had your bull been in with them?"

"Just a couple of days."

"Okay, I've got a couple of ideas."

Wyatt nodded and began striding toward the bunkhouse. He wanted to look back and see if she was watching him. He wanted to so bad; only a lifetime of self-discipline, honed to an art form by marriage to a woman who was never watching when he looked back, kept him moving the way he had to go.

⋟

Wyatt wanted to find a bed and fall face-first on it, but as he walked across the yard, a certain smell kept him on his feet.

Meat.

Wolf swung the door open to his trailer house. "Come on in and grab a burger. You've got to be starving."

Now Wyatt wanted to fall face-first on the food. He almost jogged into Wolf's house and grabbed a bun piled high with a savory meat patty, tomatoes, and onions. He nearly swallowed it whole. He ate another one while Wolf doctored up three more sandwiches.

"I'm going to run over to the bunkhouse and grab a shower. If you're planning to eat all of those, tell me now so I won't get my heart broken when I come back."

"They're yours. They'll be waiting for you."

"I don't know if they're the best thing I've ever eaten or if I'm just starving to death." Wyatt swiped another one before he left to clean up.

"Both, I reckon," Wolf said dryly.

Wyatt was in and out of the shower and back at Wolf's place in minutes. He felt 100 percent better. "I didn't realize just how deep the grit had worked into my skin." He took another burger and ate it before he sat down.

Wolf put a plate on the table in front of Wyatt. He loaded two more burgers on it and a mountain of fried potatoes. He tossed an ear of sweet corn on the plate and set a dish of melted butter and a glass of iced tea on the table. He set a plate with more burgers in the center and brought along an empty plate for himself.

Wyatt was eating before Wolf sat down. "I didn't realize how hungry I was either."

"Tough day," Wolf said.

Wyatt chewed for a while, thinking of the day Jessica died. "I reckon I've had one that was tougher."

Wolf sat across the battered wooden table.

Wyatt felt Wolf watching him eat with strange intensity. "What is it?" Wyatt braced himself for more bad news.

"So, you really like the burgers. . . ."

"Yeah. They're great. Best I've ever had." Wyatt wasn't just saying that. Now that he'd finished three of them and half the potatoes, his starving belly wasn't screaming anymore. He could actually taste them. "They're different. What'd you do to 'em?"

"You mean you want to swap recipes, Mary Lou?" Wolf's black eyes sparkled.

Wyatt almost laughed. "That's about what I'm reduced to after today. Maybe after that, you can tell me if these pants make my butt look big."

Wolf laughed and grabbed a burger for himself. "It's a buffalo burger."

Wyatt stopped with his mouth almost ready to chomp the first bite out of his fifth burger. "This is buff? Really?"

"Yep."

A thousand questions ran through Wyatt's mind, and only exhaustion made him quit sorting around for the right one. He just said what was on his mind at the moment. "Does Buffy know you're eating her herd?"

Wolf started laughing. Unfortunately he had a mouthful of buffalo, and he almost choked to death.

Wyatt ate his sandwich more carefully.

Wolf finally was breathing right again. "That's not the question I expected, but I guess I should have known you'd think of her first."

Wyatt didn't like the strange tone or the sharp way Wolf studied him. He'd known Wolf ever since the Commons had popped up next door to him over ten years ago. Wolf had gotten along well with his dad, and Wyatt had always liked him, even if he didn't like his herd or what Leonard did to the price of land.

"You know," Wolf said thoughtfully, "Buffy and I have a very different idea about what a buffalo commons should be."

"The whole Midwest, empty of people and overrun by buff, just like in the good old days," Wyatt said sarcastically.

"Not exactly what I meant. I've known her a couple of weeks, and already I've learned that she thinks with stars in her eyes. She sees these animals and sees beauty and strength, and it touches something primitive in her. Still, she's got a practical head in charge of her romantic heart. She just loves them and wants to be near them. She's done the schooling and burned off a good share of her youth working toward her goal."

"You've known her for the same length of time I have. You don't know anything about her." Wyatt grabbed a sixth burger and worked on the stack of potatoes.

Wolf poured him another glass of tea. "But I'm a different story. I don't have the heart of a practical dreamer. I have the heart of a Sioux warrior. I see buff. I see food."

"Does *Leonard* know you're eating his herd?"

Wolf laughed again. "Leonard and I almost understand each other."

"Almost?"

"Leonard isn't what he seems."

"A spoiled, rich East Coast liberal who says the right thing in front of the television cameras then does exactly what he wants in private?"

Wolf seemed amused by that. "Okay, he's *exactly* what he seems. He's got the rest of the world fooled, but I should have known better than to underestimate you."

"So, what do you mean, almost? What doesn't Leonard understand?"

Wolf said thoughtfully, "He likes the idea of being an environmentalist because it's popular. It's his cause. He doesn't have a clue what it means, but he *hires* people to understand, and he hires the best, like Buffy, like me. So he's doing good, I think."

Wyatt thought of his ruined ranch and his herd, maybe ruined. He set the buffalo burger down. His appetite was gone.

Wolf was a smart guy. He had to notice Wyatt's change in attitude, but he kept on trying to explain. "The thing he doesn't understand is that the Buffalo Commons can't survive as a rich man's toy. He's raising a herd of buffalo so big that, if something happens to him, if his heirs don't share his ideas of how to spend the family money, or if the stock market crashes, he's got a huge herd of big, dangerous animals with nowhere to go. He spends a fortune on staff and fence. He flies in and tosses big checks around and sends us every specialist we need. But the Commons can't survive like that."

"And you think you know a way to make it survive?"

Wolf gave him a long look. "I'd say you got right to the heart of the matter."

"So what's your idea?"

"It's simple. You're eating my idea. Buff weren't put on this earth to be admired and cosseted like Buffy wants to do. They were put on the earth to be part of the food chain. If Leonard would give me a year to run this place like I want, I could make it pay. I'd start by making buff into a delicacy that people would buy for special occasions, and then I'd turn it into a staple as common as hamburger. If this place could support itself, we wouldn't need Leonard's money."

"Why buffalo, Wolf? This meat is good, but it's no better than beef. And beef cattle are nowhere near as dangerous to handle or as hard to fence in."

"Yeah, but buff naturally thrive out here. They don't need the babying."

Wyatt knew that for a fact. "They're hardy, but my Angus do okay."

"They need more water, better grass, and more doctoring than a buff ever would."

"But buff will never be safe. There's no taming them and nothing except a million dollars in fence that'll keep 'em in."

"I haven't figured out the fence yet. The fence is the thing that keeps stopping me."

"But it would be solved if you could really create a buffalo commons, right?" Wyatt asked coldly. "Forget the fence and let the buffalo have the whole Great Plains."

"If I had my way, I'd use the Missouri River for the east fence and the Rockies for the west fence. I'd turn 'em loose." Wolf held up his hand to stop Wyatt. "I know that's impossible."

"My great-grandfather—"

"I know. He homesteaded this land. It's in your blood. I've heard it all. Big deal."

"Big deal?" Wyatt had taken one more bite of burger, and it was his turn to choke. He had to chew for a moment, and while he did, he studied Wolf. He had known Wolf for a long time, and he'd never seen the almost mystical calm in the man waver. Until now. Suddenly he could see the Sioux warrior. He could imagine Wolf, riding wild across the prairie, ramming a spear into a charging buffalo.

"You heard me. Big deal. My great-great-grandfather is buried under these hills. This is sacred land to my people since before recorded history. All my ancestors lived and died in these mountains and valleys. Why is your four generations of family something I should respect when you don't respect the blood that calls out to me from these hills?"

"You know I respect you, Wolf. But it's a little late to be re-fighting the Battle of the Little Big Horn. I'm here. You're here. Why isn't that enough? Why does your plan have to include me moving east of the Missouri?"

"I'll tell you why, Wyatt. It's because I've never heard you say I have a right to be here. You've wanted these buff gone from the first day they unloaded the truck."

Wyatt took a deep breath. It burned him to admit Wolf was right. He couldn't bring himself to say it now. "Now's a bad time to try and convince me these buffalo are a good idea."

Wolf snorted. "When is there ever a good time with you?"

Wyatt had to give him that one, too. "You really think you can make it pay?"

Wolf hesitated.

Wyatt saw the blazing eyes of the warrior subside. He reached for another burger.

"Now that the fence is here, yes, I think it could pay. I've even made some contacts with specialty meat buyers. I could start supplying them with buffalo meat with a phone call. I've approached Leonard about it. He lets a few buff be sold off for meat when they're injured or older, but that's not the best meat. The best is young, tender. Like what you're eating right now. Leonard lets me buy one for my own use from time to time. I'd try and get Buffy to have a bite if she wasn't a vegetarian." Wolf shook his head. "I've never figured that one out. The whole animal world eats each other, but we're not supposed to join in. It don't make sense."

Wyatt drained his glass of tea and stood up. "You've finally said something we agree on. I think we'd better go to sleep while we're ahead."

Wolf laughed and turned back to his burger. He looked at it thoughtfully. "A million dollars' worth of fence. What am I supposed to do about that?"

❧

Buffy rolled out of bed when the alarm rang at five thirty.

She almost dropped to her knees.

She groaned and would have lowered herself back into bed if she wasn't afraid she'd never get out again. Every muscle in her body was screaming at her for yesterday. She staggered to the shower, even though she'd showered last night before she went to bed. She let hot water blast down on her muscles, and it helped enough to keep her going. She swallowed more than her share of aspirin and pulled on her work clothes. She was outside at the buffalo pens long before light.

The sun peaked over the horizon just as Wolf emerged from his trailer. Wyatt and Seth came out of the bunkhouse at the same time.

She glanced at them and went back to counting buff. "Coffee in the thermos." She pointed to it and some coffee cups on the hood of her truck and went back to counting.

None of them spoke to her beyond "Morning." They just poured coffee and started their own count.

The buffalo stood or lay on the dewy grass. They weren't agitated like they'd been yesterday, which made counting easy. The day was already hot.

The heat and Buffy's movement eased the ache in her muscles

more than the shower and the aspirin. They had ten sturdy yards close around the ranch yard, and they'd divided the herd up so the number was manageable.

Buffy marked the number in the tally book, counting each pen until she got the same number twice. She was done and adding up the totals on her pocket calculator when Wyatt joined her. They compared numbers.

Wolf walked over. "We just had a good count a few weeks ago, when all the spring calving was done. They're all here."

Buffy stretched her back, and a mild groan of pain escaped.

Wyatt ran his knuckles up and down Buffy's spine. She appreciated the gesture. Too bad it was coming from a man who wished her buffalo had all died.

One of the new hands Leonard had sent came tearing into the yard in a pickup and jumped out of his cab. He hit the ground running. "We've got trouble on the west fence."

Buffy stepped past Wyatt and Wolf. "What trouble?"

"We've been putting this down as an accident—the lightning spooked the herd, and they stampeded through the fence. I've just had a closer look, and that fence was cut."

Wyatt stepped up beside her. "Deliberately cut? Someone let these buffalo loose?"

"And stampeded them, I'm guessing. It looks like fireworks were set off, aimed right at them. We found shredded Roman candles and other trash. There are tire tracks all over out there, and I found this."

It was a mirror from the side of a car. The word SUBARU was painted on the base.

"Where'd you find it?" Wyatt took the mirror. He plucked some long hairs off. Buffalo hair.

"It was in the Commons, inside the yard. There were no other tracks."

"So someone driving this rig"—Wyatt waved the mirror—"did

this? It doesn't make sense. No one's this stupid."

Buffy took the mirror and turned it over in her hands. "Someone is."

Wyatt leaned down until his nose almost touched her. He said through clenched teeth, "So now I have to deal with vandalism? Which means this could happen again?"

"The fireworks sound like the work of kids. We'll beef up security on the fence and worry about who did it when we've cleaned up the mess from the stampede. For now, just let it go." She turned away.

Wyatt caught her arm and turned her back.

"Please, Wyatt. Not now. We have the rest of our lives to argue."

Wyatt was suddenly not breathing fire. His eyes were still hot on her, but it was a different kind of heat.

Wolf said, "C'mon, Seth, we've got a fence to fix."

Buffy and Wyatt stared at each other.

Finally Wyatt said, "Do we?"

"Do we what?" She couldn't remember her name, let alone understand the question.

"Do we have the rest of our lives to argue?" His hand relaxed on her arm, but he didn't let her go.

She could have pulled free, but she didn't.

"Wyatt, I didn't know you were here."

Buffy's eyes fell closed at the sound of Jeanie's breathless pleasure. She wrenched her arm away from Wyatt. "Maybe she'll make you some breakfast. Oh, wait, she might break a nail."

Jeanie was hurrying toward them, coming out to the buffalo pens for the first time since they'd moved. "Why don't you come in and have coffee with me?"

Wyatt looked from Buffy only after Jeanie stepped between them.

"Hi, Wyatt." Jeanie ran a finger down the snapped front of his blue denim shirt.

Buffy refused to give in to her urge to protect the big lummox.

Jeanie latched onto his arm with her well-polished claws.

Buffy pulled her work gloves from behind her belt buckle and began jerking them on. "Enjoy your visit. Some of us have work to do."

ten

Buffy wondered how long Wyatt had stayed having coffee...or whatever...with Jeanie.

Buffy knew what she was doing around buffalo. It was only with people that she was a complete moron. She walked into the kitchen to find Jeanie fiddling with rabbit ears on their little TV.

With a disgruntled glance over her shoulder, Jeanie said, "I can't get anything."

"What's that you're watching now?" The television seemed to be working fine to Buffy.

"It's just regular TV. There's no cable out here, and there's a satellite out back, but Wolf said the last guy here disconnected it because he never watched TV."

"Jeanie, you haven't been bothering Wolf, have you?" Buffy imagined Wolf dodging buffalo horns while trying to appease Jeanie.

Jeanie turned the set off with a discontented *snap*. "I just asked him a few questions. I can't ask you. You're never around."

"I'll be able to help you once we clear up this mess with the stampede." Buffy went to the refrigerator, hoping for a sandwich. She saw the rest of the egg salad she'd made yesterday had been eaten. There weren't any more eggs, so an omelet was out. There were cold cuts and several packages of hamburger. There was Coke and enough junk food to live on for a week, if she didn't mind dying young.

Buffy clenched her jaw. She knew she should just eat a ham sandwich and leave. She didn't really think it was a sin

131

or anything. It was just so much healthier to eat her way, and she couldn't help picturing the pig. What really burned her was that Jeanie had done this deliberately. Just more hostility.

"There's nothing wrong with the food in there. Eat it or go without." Jeanie turned her back with a little "humph" of annoyance and went back to the TV.

Buffy saw red. "I earn the money you spent on that food!"

Jeanie rounded on her. "I get child support checks from Michael."

"You never chip any of it in to supporting us. You don't even buy things for Sally!" Buffy started looking in the cupboards for something to eat, a can of tomato soup or anything. She found cookies, snack cakes, potato chips, sugary cereal. Row after row of food that would give her a sugar high for the next hour then leave her feeling sick all afternoon.

"If you think you're so much better of a mother than I am, why don't you just say so!"

"Well, I couldn't be much worse! I'm working twenty-hour days, and I still spend more quality time with her than you do!"

"You didn't even see her yesterday!"

"I was gone in the middle of the night, and I didn't get to bed until almost midnight. And I did *so* see her. I came in for lunch, which Wyatt's niece made. And Anna kept Sally while you went to town. And you were gone for hours."

"I met someone and got to talking." Jeanie's eyes shifted in a way that worried Buffy.

"Met someone? Who?"

"None of your business. Just someone who's sick of living in the wilderness like me. I wasn't gone that long."

What was Jeanie up to? A boyfriend? Buffy hoped not, because Jeanie was still married and she'd taken no steps to divorce Michael. "If Anna hadn't been here, I'd have spent the whole day with her. And today I've been up since five thirty working, and you don't even have lunch ready! Did you feed Sally yet today?"

Jeanie ignored the question. "So you haven't seen her today. Who do you think takes care of her while you're out and about?"

Buffy had a sick feeling that Sally fended for herself. Buffy finally spotted a jar of peanut butter. "Did you at least get some bread?"

Jeanie ignored her.

Buffy opened a few drawers until she found a loaf of plain white bread. No fiber. No whole grain. With a poorly concealed growl, she made herself a peanut butter sandwich and drank a glass of milk. At least it didn't take her long.

She ate three sandwiches before the gnawing in her stomach subsided. Then she sat and nursed her second glass of milk. She pictured Jeanie clinging to Wyatt's arm and felt a pang of guilt because she was afraid her temper had at least a little—oh all right, a *lot*—to do with that. Jeanie had taken Michael's desertion hard, and it had changed her. She was still healing, and Buffy had agreed to give her time.

Buffy drained the glass of milk then tried one more time. "I do think you should be in here with Sally. And I know she's a handful."

Jeanie didn't turn, but she said quietly, "It's all meaningless without Mike. I can't seem to care about anything. I know I don't help like I should, but. . ." Jeanie shrugged and turned around. Her eyes were bleak, like a child who had become separated from her parent in a shopping mall. She was lost and too scared to think.

It broke Buffy's heart just as it had been breaking her heart for the last year, but she'd babied her sister long enough. "You have to go back to the grocery store and get something so I can eat a quick meal. I need you to do that for me."

Buffy tugged her tally book out of her breast pocket. She quickly wrote a short list of food she wanted on hand. Jeanie's face took on a mulish look, but Buffy ignored it. "I expect this list to be filled today. And I shouldn't have to write the list. You know what I like to eat. You deliberately bought things I didn't like. It's time to grow up. If I earn the money, you take care of the house and the meals and Sally. That means have a hot dinner waiting tonight."

Buffy held her sister's eyes until Jeanie looked away. Buffy knew Jeanie was no match for her when it came to being strong-willed. But Buffy hated to browbeat her. "And take Sally with you to the store. I can't watch her today."

"I might stop by Wyatt's house," Jeanie said. "If I found someone to marry me, I'd be out from under your feet."

Buffy suppressed a pang of jealousy. "You're already married. You can't start a relationship with a man until you've finished things with Michael."

Jeanie had twice her skill with men. She'd always been able to pick and choose when they were teenagers, while Buffy had been the studious, buffalo-loving geek who was two years younger than her classmates. And Jeanie liked strong men, which Buffy didn't. If Jeanie wanted Wyatt, she could probably have him.

"If you decide you want Wyatt, you'd better be prepared to live out here for the rest of your life. There are no malls, no movies, no dress shops. And he'll expect you to take care of Sally and both of his boys and have three hot meals a day waiting for him. Plus you'll have to garden, tend his chickens, and probably ride herd on his cattle. So don't set your sights on the man unless you want the whole package. That's not fair to him or you."

Jeanie studied her shrewdly. Buffy suspected Jeanie was using what she knew about her little sister to read between the lines.

"I think I'll just go ahead and stop by anyway, but thanks for the advice."

Buffy slapped the short list on the table. "Suit yourself." She almost ran out of the house to keep herself from saying, "Leave Wyatt alone. He's mine," or "I love him," or something equally ridiculous. Except as she thought it, she knew it was true. She didn't know him that well, and what she did know, she mostly didn't like. But there was no denying the feeling in her heart. And there was no way she could ever act on that love.

She went hunting for the peace she always felt with her buffalo, even though they were domineering and stubborn and dangerous. As she walked toward the pens, it occurred to her that Wyatt was domineering and stubborn and more than a little bit dangerous. Good grief, she'd fallen in love with a buffalo!

She would bet anything the man was incapable of feeling any soft emotions at all.

❧

Wyatt sat on the front porch of his house and looked at the ruin of his ranch and wanted to cry.

The boys came outside and climbed into his lap, strangely subdued even considering the circumstances.

"Are you sure Gumby's going to be all right, Dad?" Cody asked, resting his head on Wyatt's chest.

Wyatt ran his hand through Cody's unruly dark curls, so like his own. "Yes, Wolf said he's okay. He's got a badly hurt leg, and we won't be able to ride him for a while, but we'll baby him, and he'll heal."

Wyatt was getting the biggest machine shed Morton made. A work crew was cleaning up the yard. The local Ford dealer was bringing out a brand-new car for Anna and a new truck for Wyatt. A planeload of veterinarians had come out to check Wyatt's herd and decide how to handle the threat of disease and pregnancy. An assessor was wandering around the ranch, studying the premises with his sharpened pencil and Mr. Leonard's checkbook.

Wyatt wanted to punch the guy in the face and suggest he pass that along to Leonard.

"It's going to be okay, Uncle Wyatt."

Wyatt glanced sideways at Anna as she emerged from the house. Even with the new car on the way, she still had that same flash of rage in her eyes. He knew he'd been complaining about the buffalo too loud for too long. Now this happened, and maybe Anna really did need money for pain and suffering. Maybe she needed counseling to get past this.

He reached out an arm to where she stood in the doorway and pulled her close to him and the boys. "I guess I'm in shock or something. I can't seem to think of anything to do but sit."

Some of the anger faded from her eyes. "The cleaning crew is almost done, and the new carpet is in. They said the new window will arrive later today and they'll have it installed by quitting time."

Wyatt thought about the stampede and the danger of having his boys in a room with an outside door, not that the little imps weren't fully capable of climbing out an upstairs window and escaping if they took the notion. "I've decided I'm going to move downstairs and let the boys have my room."

"Why, Dad? The front room is bigger. We want the biggest because we're two and you're only one."

"I've just decided is all. You'll be closer to the bathroom up there. My room's not the biggest room, but it's big enough. It'll work okay."

The boys, who argued about everything, accepted his decision. Colt finally stood up and said, "Let's go do it. I don't want to look anymore."

Wyatt said, "Sounds good to me. I'll bet if I ask that cleaning crew to help, they'll jump right to it. All these people seem real worried about me being upset. We can get that room moved in a few minutes."

They had the whole thing done in half an hour, and Wyatt got in the swing of being a human being again. Then Buffy's truck pulled into his driveway. He saw it from his upstairs window, where his room was now filled with toy guns and Matchbox cars. All his lethargy evaporated, and he thought of a dozen things he could go argue about. He jogged down the stairs and stormed out on the porch, eager for another round.

Then he saw Jeanie's blond hair, and his spirits sank even further into his boots, where they'd been all day. Ever since he'd quit arguing with Buffy this morning.

Great. Just what he needed. Perky.

He went to the door and yelled up the stairs, "Anna, boys! Get out here!"

He hadn't thought of needing a buffer zone until he'd recognized the leech.

eleven

A week later, Wyatt stared at the huge steel machine shed going up on top of the memory of his grandpa's barn. It was a beautiful building. It was going to be of far more use to him than his old red barn.

Then he looked down at the check in his hand. A quarter of a million dollars. He wanted to crush it. Rip it to pieces. Burn it. Tell Leonard what he could do with his hush money. Instead, with bitter self-derision, he climbed into the new Ford 350 monster pickup truck Leonard had delivered from a dealer in Hot Springs and drove to Cold Creek to put the check in the bank. Then he came home in his one-ton black monster truck, with a four-door crew cab—every toy a man ever dreamed of.

Leonard had even paid for five years' worth of insurance on the overpriced beast. It was easily the most expensive rig in the county, and Wyatt felt like a fool driving it.

There was a brand-new Mustang in the yard at home for Anna. Leonard had offered a Porsche, but Anna's parents had refused to let their daughter drive such a powerful car. They'd agreed to let her accept the Mustang with a state-of-the-art CD player and in the color of her choice—red. Then Leonard's assessor offered the rest of the value of a Porsche in cash. Anna had started yelling and crying, so the guy promised her a hefty check for her pain and suffering and said he was sending it to her parents with or without her approval.

Wyatt didn't know what would be the point in refusing the money. Still, he was a sellout, and all the horsepower in the world under his mammoth Ford hood wouldn't change that.

Then, in the midst of his self-contempt, a wild hair had him turning toward the Buffalo Commons. He hadn't seen Buffy in a week, and that gave him a strange itch he didn't understand. He only knew seeing Buffy would scratch it.

❧

He pulled into the Commons, and the first thing he saw was Buffy perched precariously on top of the corral timbers.

The buffalo were being let out of the sturdy pens for the first time since the stampede. They were wandering in their lazy way out into the pasture. Wyatt's gut twisted as he thought of all those big animals loose again.

Buffy swung around as he neared her. She looked straight at him with those warm brown eyes, in a way that made Wyatt wonder if she didn't have some special radar where he was concerned. Or maybe he just clomped when he walked.

She looked past him to his truck and arched her eyebrows. "Those're some mean wheels, Wyatt. Compliments of Mr. Leonard?"

"He didn't even ask me what kind. He just had the biggest one on the planet driven out to my place with the license and registration already in my name. I'm embarrassed to be seen driving it."

Buffy laughed. It was a deep, throaty laugh, and it was the first time he'd heard it, although she'd laughed more mildly at the boys' antics that first day. He knew if he started yelling, she'd certainly quit laughing.

Still, a man had to say what was on his mind. "Would you mind coming down off that fence?"

"I think I'll stay here. If I get down there, you'll tower over me, and I don't like that."

"Buffy," Wyatt barked, "get down now!"

She smiled at him then shrugged her shoulders. "Why not."

She swung her legs to Wyatt's side of the fence and jumped

to the ground, landing with the grace of an Olympic gymnast. She dusted the seat of her pants and yelled over her shoulder, "I'll take the first watch, Wolf. We need men on that fence all night. Break it down to four two-hour shifts."

"Already done. You want to take the truck or a horse?"

"I'll drive my truck." Buffy turned back to Wyatt. "Let's go have a look at that hot rod you're driving." She began walking toward the truck, and Wyatt followed along reluctantly.

"Okay, we're out of earshot; what did you want to yell at me about?" Buffy asked.

"I didn't come over here to yell at you."

"Oh sure you did. I've missed it anyway. I'd have probably come over there and insulted your political party or gun owners or something precious to you for sure, just to get a fix."

"I did *not* come over here to yell. I just wanted to know what's being done about the lunatics who cut your fence."

Buffy shoved her hands into the back pockets of her blue jeans. "It's out of my hands. Mr. Leonard's people are looking into it."

"Have you called the police?"

Buffy shook her head. "Not since that first night. I left that to Mr. Leonard's people at his specific instructions."

"So the county sheriff hasn't even been out?" Wyatt got to the truck and opened the driver's side door for Buffy to look in.

Buffy stared at the rig. "Good grief, the seat is as high as my nose."

"Has he been out?" Wyatt demanded.

Buffy turned from the truck to face Wyatt. "He called one day. I referred him to the phone number Mr. Leonard gave me. I've never heard back."

He reluctantly admired her guts as she stonewalled him about something that was life and death. "So nothing is being done," Wyatt said flatly.

"I can't answer that. I don't know what's being done."

Wyatt leaned close to her. She was filthy dirty again and dripping with sweat. He rested his hands on her waist and hoisted her onto his seat.

She squeaked with surprise and steadied herself by grabbing his forearms.

He jerked his head. "Scoot over. I'll take you for a ride."

"I don't have time to go for a ride. You heard me tell Wolf I'd take the first watch."

He shoved her across the seat. "This won't take long, but I'd like some privacy."

"What for?" Buffy slid, and Wyatt scaled the truck.

"Because you're right after all." Wyatt twisted the key, and the rig roared instantly to life.

"About what?" Buffy clung to her door which left about an acre of space between them.

"I do want to yell at you." Wyatt jammed the truck into gear and laid a path of dust a half mile long as he tore out of the driveway.

Buffy had her fingers clasped on the door handle as Wyatt did his best to give her whiplash. He wondered if he might have scared her, but a glance at her expression told him she was impatient and annoyed but a long way from scared. Drat it.

"As long as we're not headed anywhere specific, let's drive out to the spot where the fence was cut. I want another look."

"Have you investigated at all? The police could be tracking down that Subaru. How many can there be in that shade of green?"

"The truth is, Wyatt, I think Mr. Leonard is trying to make this whole thing go away. I have gotten a few calls from the press. A couple of radio stations in Rapid City called and one in Pierre. They said they'd gotten a tip. I said," Buffy's voice went all Southern-belle fake, and she fluttered her eyelashes, " 'Why, whatever do you mean? We don't have any buffalo out.'"

Wyatt smiled at the phoniness.

"It was the truth, since we had them all back in when the calls came. They accepted my answer like it was what they expected to hear. Even though everyone around here knows about it, there wasn't a word about it in the local paper. Even if someone does go to the press about it now, there's not much to tell. It's all cleaned up."

"Leonard is good." Wyatt quit driving like a maniac and steered along the fence line, passing the stretched-out line of ambling buffalo. "He never told me the money was on the condition I not talk. He knew I'd refuse. But he also made the settlement so generous that it's embarrassing. I mean, here I am, driving this dumb truck. How much is anyone going to listen if I claim I've been hurt?"

"Is the new machine shed going up?" Buffy relaxed her death grip on the door handle and turned to him.

"Yes, and it's beautiful. It's even going to have a heated office."

They drove in silence that was broken by the deep-throated roar of Wyatt's high-powered truck engine. Wyatt finally reached the far end of the pasture and slowed as he drove along the reinforced fence.

"Stop here!" Buffy said suddenly. "I can still see the tracks. I want to have a closer look."

Wyatt pulled his truck to a stop and climbed out.

Buffy had to get out of her seat like she was riding a slippery slide. Even with the running board, it was a long way down.

Buffy started toward the tracks, and Wyatt fell in beside her. She went down on one knee beside a particularly deep rut. "I don't know anything about tire marks, but these are clear enough. Someone should take a picture of it or a molding. It could be used to double-check that this is the same car that lost the side mirror. We don't know how many people were in on this."

Wyatt looked up from the tire marks and studied the landscape around them. He pointed toward a rise. "If anyone was scouting your property, they'd watch from up there. And there's an underground spring that makes that whole hillside soft. There might be more tracks."

Buffy rose. "Surely some of Leonard's people have looked into it."

"It doesn't matter if they have or not." Wyatt went back to his truck. "That hill doesn't belong to Mr. Leonard. It's on Shaw land. And if they're trespassing on my land to scout an attack on the Buffalo Commons, then they don't just have a problem with Leonard. They've got a problem with me."

Buffy looked away from the hill as she walked beside him to the truck. "And having a problem with a rancher is worse than having a problem with a multibillionaire?"

Wyatt narrowed his eyes as he looked at her. "What do you think?"

"I think I'm more interested in getting to the bottom of this than Leonard is. I think I'd like to see what's on top of that hill."

Wyatt jerked his head in a nod of approval. He swung up to the seat as she got in her side. He slammed the door. "The minute this is over, I'm trading this stupid thing in for two reasonable trucks."

"Sounds good."

Wyatt grinned. He'd been right to come and see Buffy. He hadn't felt this good in. . .six and a half days. He headed up the gentle slope of the highest hill around.

≈

Buffy said, "Will you look at that?"

Wyatt stopped his truck.

Buffy jerked open her door and rushed over to the obvious campsite. It wasn't just a couple of tire tracks. The ground was torn up until there was hardly any grass. Buffy felt her temper explode. "Leonard's men didn't even look around! No one could miss this!"

Buffy crouched by the fire and reached for a scrap of paper that was burned around the edges. She pulled her hand back. "Wyatt!"

He was beside her instantly. "What?"

"These ashes are still hot!"

Wyatt crouched beside her and held his hand close to the campfire. "They didn't leave after the stampede. They're still around."

Buffy grabbed his arm. "They're not done. They're planning another attack!"

Wyatt studied the horizon in all directions.

"So where do you hide in these hills?" Buffy pulled the scrap of paper out of the fire. She stared at it, and her gut twisted. "My name?"

Wyatt took the paper. "It doesn't mean anything. They probably just know you run the place."

Buffy leaned closer and tried to figure out why her name had given her such a jolt. Then she got it. "My name. . .in Jeanie's handwriting."

Wyatt looked at Buffy, and she saw the compassion in his eyes. "She might not know what they're really up to. Maybe she just talked to someone, gave them information without realizing what they'd use it for."

But Buffy had seen Jeanie's anger. "I haven't told you all that's gone on at the Commons this week."

"Like what?" Wyatt asked, watching her closely.

Buffy ran one hand through her hair. "Jeanie's been going to town a lot. Leaving Sally with me and spending late afternoons and evenings in Cold Creek. Only I checked my truck, and she's piling up too many miles. I'd decided she had a boyfriend somewhere, but. . ."

Wyatt crumpled the scrap of paper in his fist. "She couldn't be involved. Not after she came to my place. She saw the burned-out shells of my truck and Anna's car. She saw the rubble where my barn used to be."

"Whether Jeanie's in it or not, someone is definitely planning something," Buffy snapped. "If they've got another attack planned and Jeanie knows about it, I'm going to find out. Let's go back to the Commons." She stood and turned to the truck.

"Wait," Wyatt said, looking down the hill away from the Commons. "I think I know where they might be."

Buffy caught his arm and pulled. "We've got to get back. I still have time to round the buffalo up and put them back in the pens. Whoever did this has obviously been watching the Commons. They might plan on striking as soon as the buff are loose. That's now!"

"There's a deserted house just off the edge of my property. It's not that far from here as the crow flies. These tracks even head in that direction."

"It's getting dark. If we miss them, we won't be in time to stop the attack."

"Then we'd better hurry." Wyatt strong-armed her into the truck.

Buffy let herself be manhandled. They disagreed on how to handle it, but they both wanted to act. "Do you have a CB in this carnival ride?"

Wyatt said grimly, "Nope. Everything else in the universe but."

Buffy said, "Let's get over to that house and find out if they're there. If they're not, I need to get back to the Commons and get those buffalo back in the pens."

Wyatt bounced his truck down the hill. It was getting dark,

and he managed to hit every rut and rock. He glanced at Buffy. "What's the point in having a heavy-duty pickup if you don't abuse it?"

Buffy fastened her seat belt after her head hit the roof. "Slow down. I want to get there in one piece."

Wyatt kept pushing, and they rounded the last hillock to see the outline of a mansion in the encroaching dusk.

"Good grief, who built that?"

"We call it the Barrett Place. The old folks are dead and gone, and their kids moved to the city. My dad bought the land, but the Barrett family kept the house and a few acres around it for some reason. Sentimental, I guess. It's falling in."

"It's spectacular." The house was three stories, a Victorian dream house full of elaborate rooflines and gingerbread accents.

Wyatt drove around to a shed. Empty. "Look at the tracks. They're definitely using this place." He pulled up to the house, got out, and strode to the back door, which hung on one hinge. Wyatt swung the door open, and it fell flat on the floor.

"There's no one here." Buffy peeked over his shoulder. "Let's go. I've got to get back to the Commons. And this time, I'm going to handle this without calling Leonard."

They ran for the truck, and Wyatt drove like a madman.

Buffy rubbed a hand over her face and tried to deny the possibility that her sister had sold her out to a stranger who offered her a strong shoulder.

twelve

"Here he comes. The moron didn't even turn his headlights off until just a minute ago." Wolf wired the last pen shut on the secured buffalo. He sent the men up and down the length of the pens to stop the oncoming car.

"What if he doesn't stop?" Buffy sat in Wyatt's megatruck, facing the intruders.

"He'll stop." Wyatt nodded to Wolf and began driving forward slowly, his lights off, his motor running as slowly as possible so they could pick up any night sounds. "He's a coward, remember? As soon as he sees that there's someone around, he'll try to hightail it. But we're not letting him out of here."

Buffy clutched Wyatt's strong arm, surprised at how good it felt to have someone to depend on. "Thanks for getting Anna and the boys over here. I can't believe Jeanie left Sally asleep alone in the house."

Wyatt looked at her, his hazel eyes flashing in the dashboard lights. "Let's stop here and wait for them. There's no sense going out any farther. They might get past us in the dark." Wyatt stopped the truck. When he switched off the motor, the sound of an approaching vehicle was audible. "Tell me what she said in her note again."

"She said she's leaving for good and not to hunt for her. The note gives me the right to adopt Sally. I know it's not a legal document, but it still shows her state of mind, that she wants to be done with both of us. How can she abandon her own child? Wyatt, she wasn't always like this. It's just that Michael, her husband, told her every move to make, and when he left her,

147

she just lost her anchor."

"Was he abusive?"

Buffy was startled by the question. "I've never considered that he was. If you ask Jeanie, she'll tell you they were blissfully happy."

"A lot of domineering men use their fists to enforce the rules. And a lot of women accept it."

"My dad was a tyrant, but he just yelled all the time and told every one of us how to act."

Wyatt laid his hand on her shoulder. "Let me guess. Military? An army drill sergeant?"

"Actually he was an accountant. I think he was obsessed with making things balance at work, and that need for control just got landed right on our heads."

"And your mom put up with it?"

Buffy couldn't help but enjoy the weight of Wyatt's hand on her shoulder. She shifted a little to get closer. "My mom always blamed herself if he yelled. Jeanie thought he was wonderful, too. I was the troublemaker. I was always defying him, and I always ended up being sent to my room. I've avoided men like him." She didn't add, "and you," but she thought it.

"So you have an accountant phobia?" Wyatt asked lightly.

That surprised a laugh out of her. "You gotta watch those CPAs."

Wyatt dragged her the last four feet across the expanse of truck seat. "Good thing I was a failure at algebra."

She didn't see his head lowering in the dark, but she felt it. She felt him. His warmth and strength. The earthy smell of hard work that was a part of him. His hands were strong and steady. His lips firm and yet gentle at the same time. She didn't feel in danger. She felt protected. And that was the greatest danger of all.

She tried to push him away and ended up with her arms

around his neck. She needed to tell him to stop but instead let the kiss deepen.

Wyatt set her firmly away. "They're coming. Get ready."

Who was coming? Get ready for what? Then she heard the motor only a few yards ahead of them and remembered why they were out here.

Wyatt gunned his truck to life and switched on his headlights. The car coming toward them stopped.

Wyatt swung his truck door open and slid to the ground.

Just as he landed, the oncoming car roared toward them. The door Wyatt had left open slammed closed brutally then tore away. The car scraped the whole driver's side of the truck. The ugly sound of metal on metal twisted Buffy's stomach. The monster truck shook but didn't move while the smaller vehicle bounced off and drove right over Wyatt.

As quickly as it had struck, the smaller car was gone, driving for the ranch yard and the herd.

"Wyatt!" Buffy scrambled to the driver's side of the rig, ready to leap out the gaping opening. She came nose to nose with Wyatt, who was rolling out from under the truck.

Wyatt shoved her across the seat. "Are you all right?"

"I'm fine."

He threw his truck into gear and spun it around in a sickening U-turn. Wind blew in from the missing door as he fumbled for the CB, which he'd scrounged from the Commons. "They're coming!"

Wolf's voice, metallic through the radio, shouted, "I heard the crash. Are you both all right?"

"Yes, but they've destroyed another truck! He slammed right into me. He's crazy. Did the sheriff ever get there?"

"He's here. He brought half the county with him. Plenty of people mad about this mess."

"I don't want any of my neighbors hurt," Wyatt said grimly.

"The driver of that car is acting like this is a suicide mission. Get everybody out of the line of fire!"

"We're ready for 'em," Wolf said.

"I'm coming right behind. I'll try and slow them down. Don't let anyone get trigger happy while we're out here."

Then the Subaru's brake lights lit up. Wyatt was closing in fast. Wyatt's new truck was far better suited to the terrain than the battered Outback.

Wyatt said, "Buckle up." He buckled his own seat belt as Buffy quickly fastened hers. Wyatt hit the brakes to slow down then rammed the back end of the Subaru. It spun sideways, and the two vehicles hit broadside, driver's sides together.

With Wyatt's door ripped away, Buffy could see into the smaller rig. She saw rage in the eyes of a young man. His car slid up on two wheels, and as if it were in slow motion, it rolled onto its side, still sliding.

Wyatt leaped from his truck. Six pairs of headlights were coming toward them from the Commons but were still a ways off.

Buffy jumped down. "Be careful."

Wyatt ran around to the other side of the car and leaned over the windshield to look inside. A plume of smoke curled up from the engine.

"Wyatt, it's on fire!"

"Get back!" Wyatt shouted.

Buffy hoped he wasn't talking to her, because no way was she leaving him. She ran around to his side and heard the screams of fear and pain coming from inside the car. Wyatt kicked the windshield out; then he kicked again to make a bigger hole and slithered into the burning vehicle on his belly.

Wolf ran up beside Buffy just as she dropped on her knees to climb in after Wyatt. He caught her around the waist and pulled her away.

Fighting the grip, she screamed, "No, I'm going after Wyatt!"

"Keep out of his way." Wolf shook her. "There's not room for two of you inside there."

Wyatt came out backward, dragging a young man with short, dark hair. The man clung to a shotgun, but Wyatt disarmed him quickly.

"Jeanie, she's in there." Blood dripped from the man's forehead as he collapsed beside the burning car. "She got thrown into the back. There are bottles of gas in there. I was going to torch the fence and the barns. They're going to blow."

Buffy lunged for the shattered window.

Wyatt caught her around the waist, and for a second, their eyes met. In that look was everything—right down to Wyatt's soul—that made him the man he was. The man she loved. He spun her away from the car and thrust her into someone else's strong arms.

Wolf's.

Then Wyatt turned back to the car.

"Stop him!"

Wolf had his arm around her like a steel band. He turned and said, "You hold her back. I'm going to help Wyatt."

Buffy felt herself handed off again. She fought against the grip as she saw Wyatt's legs vanish into the car. He needed to climb all the way to the back. He couldn't get in and drag an injured passenger out before the car exploded. She wrenched against the man, who she now saw wore a sheriff's badge.

He shouted over the crackling of the flames, "You can't help him except to stay out of the way!"

Buffy rounded on him, still clamped against his body. He dragged her away from the car as the flames began to get too hot. She twisted her head around.

Wolf scrambled, shouted, ducking past the flames, peering into the interior of the car.

Buffy suddenly knew Wyatt was out of time. She heard the

whine of something under pressure, getting ready to blow. She couldn't fight the man who restrained her any more than she could fight Wyatt or Wolf or her father. So she used her wiles. She relaxed, smiling sweetly at the big lummox who was holding her. "All right, Sheriff. I panicked there for a second, but I'm better now." She heard the shrill whine of that building pressure, but she remained calm.

The sheriff said in a patronizing voice, "I understand. Too much excitement can get a little lady all worked up."

"You're so right. But I'm okay now."

More cars pulled up.

The sheriff let her go.

She spun around and charged for the back of the Subaru. She got around to the rear of the car just as whatever was whining began screaming under the pressure.

Flames shot up higher than Wolf's head at the front of the car, and he staggered backward into the sheriff, who'd been coming after Buffy. The crackling flames drowned out their shouting.

She reached for the door latch on the back, but it burned her fingers. She dropped to the ground and kicked in the back window just as Wolf got to her side.

Wyatt was backed against the window, facing a wall of flames.

Buffy grabbed him by the back of his shirt and dragged him out of the fire.

Wyatt's pant legs were on fire, and he had Jeanie in his arms.

Wolf grabbed Jeanie, whose jacket was ablaze.

Buffy and Wolf pulled them clear.

Buffy threw herself at Wyatt's feet. Beating at the flames with her bare hands, she screamed Wyatt's name.

Wyatt coughed, nearly choking.

Wolf rolled Jeanie, unconscious, away from the fire, ripped off her jacket, and scooped dirt onto her clothes.

Wyatt yelled, "It's gonna blow. That car is full of gas cans!"

Buffy caught Wyatt around the middle and hoisted him to his feet. Then the two of them staggered away as Wolf dragged Jeanie to safety.

The gas erupted. The force of the explosion knocked everyone to the ground. Fire rained down. Everyone fought a short, brutal battle against the flames.

The flames climbed into the starlit night, but the burning cinders quit falling.

Wyatt sagged backward onto the ground.

Wolf turned to check on Jeanie.

"How bad is it?" Buffy demanded. She grabbed the bottom hem of Wyatt's blackened denim jeans and ripped them up to his knees. Heavy boots had protected him.

"I'm fine. I'm not burned." Wyatt got wearily to his feet.

She turned and dropped to her knees beside Jeanie. "Is she badly burned?"

"No." Wolf had two fingers on Jeanie's throat, checking for a pulse. "Probably inhaled too much smoke. She's breathing. Her pulse is strong. We called the ambulance when Wyatt first said you'd been hit. They'll be here pretty soon."

Buffy felt the first tears burn her eyes. She stood and threw herself into Wyatt's arms.

He stumbled backward, but he steadied himself and caught on to what she was doing right away. He kissed her. Right there in front of the blazing Subaru, the brainless kid who had made this mess, and every man and buffalo in Custer County, South Dakota.

The county men weren't so busy watching the fire that they couldn't give them a round of applause.

thirteen

Jeanie was awake before the ambulance came. She refused to look at Buffy and told her to stay away from the hospital. The county sheriff took the young man into custody and told Jeanie she would be arrested when she left the hospital.

Wyatt distracted Buffy from her anger and fear for Jeanie by asking her to marry him. This Saturday.

He wanted a wedding smaller than small. The boys and Sally and maybe Wolf, if he wasn't busy with the buffalo. They had things settled before they pulled into the yard at the Commons.

Wolf came striding over to see them.

Buffy jumped down from the truck, eager to tell Wolf they'd set a date. Before she could speak, in the bright yard light, she saw Wolf's furious anger.

"What is it?" Wyatt said before she could.

Wyatt came up beside Buffy and put his arm around her, as if he knew whatever was coming might require his support.

"We're fired!"

"We're. . .you and me?" Buffy asked.

"I got the word before we went out to catch the vandals, but I couldn't tell you while we were dealing with that mess. All of us. Seth, the men riding the fence, all the staff. We've just gotten our two weeks' notice. Leonard didn't even have the class to call himself. He had one of his aides do it."

"Then maybe it isn't right. He can't just fire everybody. Someone's got to ride herd on—"

"The Buffalo Commons is history. The stock market did one

of its dives, and Leonard is all of a sudden not such a rich man. This is one of the toys he's selling."

"But where will they go? No one wants a thousand head of buffalo. There's no one who can afford to keep them. The national parks are already fighting an overgrazing problem."

"He's already taken care of the problem. His aide told me all about it." Wolf turned to look at the buffalo pens. His fists were clenched, and Buffy thought he was imagining getting his hands on Leonard.

"How can he have? No one will buy them. He can't have solved the problem."

"Sure, someone will buy them, Buffy," Wolf said with vicious sarcasm. "Dog food companies. Leonard's gofer said he is calling them today. They'll buy them for less than the cost of trucking them to their plant. They'll start picking them up a semiload at a time in a couple of days, and that's it. Problem solved."

Buffy staggered backward. "That's not possible. He can't do that. These buffalo are—"

Wyatt caught her as her knees gave out.

"They're not an endangered species," Wolf cut in. "They're privately owned, and Leonard can do what he wants with them."

"But the press will eat him alive," Wyatt said.

Buffy said, "That's right! This would be a public relations nightmare."

"He's going broke, Buffy. He can't afford this place anymore. He's putting the land up for sale and washing his hands of the whole thing. He doesn't care about the public relations when he's fighting for his financial life."

Wyatt asked, "Do you have his number?"

Wolf turned slowly back from the pens at the tone in Wyatt's voice. "Sure. There was a time, when we were just starting this, I thought of the man as a friend."

"You have Louis Leonard's private number?" Buffy asked incredulously.

Wolf rattled off the number, and Wyatt grabbed his tally book and jotted it down. Wolf asked, "What are you thinking? Have you got an idea that could save this place?"

"I'm thinking there's a huge piece of land for sale, and I'm all of a sudden a rich man. I think Mr. Leonard and I could do some business."

"You'd sell us out like that, Shaw?" Wolf said angrily. "I wouldn't have given you the number if I'd known that!"

"Wyatt," Buffy said, "you can't do this. You can't profit by this disaster."

"Buffy, I know how much you love these buffalo." Wyatt tried to sound kind, but Buffy heard a domineering, patronizing male running roughshod over her. "I understand you—"

"You don't understand anything!" She felt her temper ignite, and she knew she should walk away. She loved Wyatt, but right now, she might say something she'd regret.

Then he patted her on the shoulder like she was a fussy child.

Her temper blew. "You can't take away the thing I love most in the world and expect to have a future with me!"

Wyatt's expression hardened. "I thought I was the thing you loved most in the world."

"Wyatt, don't do this," Wolf said. "We've been friends, but—"

"You, too, Wolf?" Wyatt sounded almost hurt. With cold sarcasm, he said, "And here I thought you might be willing to work with me once the Commons was gone."

"As your hired man, Wyatt?" Wolf sneered. "I don't need a job so bad I'd work with a traitor."

Wyatt's jaw clenched until his mouth was one angry straight line. "I think you should know me a little better than that, Wolf. I think, after all these years, you should trust me."

Buffy tried to calm down. "Wyatt, if we can keep anyone from buying the ranch, maybe Leonard will at least wait to sell the buffalo until we can find a buyer. There are a lot of small animal parks who would buy them five or ten at a time. But if you step in with an offer, he'll grab it and send in the semis."

"And you, Buffy"—Wyatt turned on her—"you have told me a dozen times, a hundred times, that you love buffalo. I respect that, but I thought you loved me, too. I would have hoped to at least be in a tie with them. I would have hoped maybe Sally might rank above them, even if I didn't. I know how independent and strong you are, and those are things I love about you."

Buffy could hear Wyatt's temper building until it reached a flash point. "So now it comes down to this—the buffalo or trusting the man you said you loved. Why am I so surprised you picked the buffalo? How could I have ever fooled myself into believing you'd do it any other way?"

Wyatt tugged his Stetson down until it nearly covered his eyes and took a long, hard look at the phone number in his hand. "Enjoy Yellowstone. I've got a phone call to make." He turned and moved away with his usual fluid grace.

Buffy reached her hand out, knowing her only chance for love was walking away. She had seen his hurt, but as usual, he reacted with anger. He was going home to destroy her dreams.

Wolf fumed beside her, the buffalo snuffled in the darkness, and Wyatt drove out of the yard in his battered black truck without spinning a wheel or throwing up a single piece of gravel. Cold. Controlled. Domineering.

Everything she didn't want, wrapped up in the man of her dreams.

fourteen

Leonard called her the next morning and woke Buffy up.

She was still trying to get the phone centered on her ear when Leonard said, "I can't get ahold of Wolf, so you pass the word on. I've sold the place to Wyatt Shaw."

"No!"

"He bought the buffalo, too," Leonard announced with his usual high energy.

Her confused heart mended a bit. "Mr. Leonard, you sold the buffalo to Wyatt? Why did he want—"

"I gave them to him. The dog food company wasn't going to pay much. By the time I paid for trucking, it was going to be a wash. As Wyatt pointed out, this way is better PR, and it's chump change considering my financial situation. Getting out from under the tax burden is worth it. He wants all of you to stay on and work at the Commons, but he's going to run it his way. He said you're headed to Yellowstone, so he'll hire someone new or just leave Wolf in charge. He doesn't care much about college degrees."

Buffy stammered, "Wyatt doesn't like buffalo. He'd never—"

"The sale is final. I've got a full morning. Take it up with your new boss." The phone clicked in her ear.

Buffy stared at the receiver for a few blank seconds as her sleep-fogged brain tried to make sense of the abrupt call. She hung up in a daze. Then it all added up. With a squeal of delight, she threw the covers back, jumped into her clothes, and ran outside.

Wolf was just coming out of his trailer. "Did you hear?"

158

Buffy ran up to him, smiling. "That Wyatt bought the ranch and wants to run the Commons? Yes, Leonard called me. He called you, too?"

"No." Wolf jerked his thumb at his trailer. "I just got off the phone with Wyatt. He hired me to manage the Commons. Although he said the Commons was a stupid name that insulted every rancher in the state and he was renaming it the S Bar B Ranch."

"What? He hired you?" Buffy's stomach sank as she remembered Leonard talking about her going to Yellowstone. Wyatt was already planning his life without her. "To do my job?"

"Yep, well, sort of. We're going to run things different. We're going to raise buffalo for. . ." Wolf stopped. His face took on a look that almost seemed like pity. "For meat."

"Meat?" Buffy said, aghast.

Wolf squared his shoulders and looked her in the eye. "Wyatt and I talked about it awhile back. He thinks. . .well, I think. . . we can make this ranch pay. Make buffalo into a real product that people will pay well for. I know I can get the business into the black, especially since Leonard already made all the big investments—in fence and buildings. That's what I've always wanted, and Wyatt wants to do it my way."

"Your way?" Buffy began pulling herself together. The shocks of last night. Being fired by Leonard. Being dumped by Wyatt. The fate of her beautiful buffalo herd. After she'd gotten her temper under control, she'd cried herself to sleep. Then to wake up this morning and have it all fixed. The buffalo would live. Wyatt would hire her back, and if he wanted to hire her, then he wanted her to stay. But now he was going to turn her buffalo into a food crop. Buffy got a stranglehold on her feelings and packed them into a tight little box and shoved that box into the deepest corner of her heart to be dealt with later—or better yet, forgotten altogether.

"There will be a place for you here, Buffy. If you want it. But you know the only possible way for buffalo to ever really prosper in this world is if they pay. No one can afford to do what Leonard was doing for long. We can't rely on the whims of a rich landlord to tell us if we can exist. Buffalo can either sustain themselves, or they can't. Wyatt and I are going to find out."

"So capitalism is what it's all about?" Buffy said bitterly.

Wolf looked at her coolly as if taking her measure. She didn't like it that she seemed to be coming up short. "You need to talk to Wyatt about this. I think this is a better idea than anything Leonard ever did. You can get behind this. You can be a part of this. If it works and buffalo meat really catches on, we could create a real buffalo commons. Buffalo are better suited to this land than cattle, and I think ranchers might switch to buffalo if they could see a business in it."

"I don't see where I fit into this scheme. I won't be part of turning these majestic animals into food. I'd just as soon see them go to the dog food factory. I think I'll just follow the plan I settled on last night and head for Wyoming. I can vacation in Yellowstone until it's time for my job to start."

"What about your doctoral dissertation? Isn't it based on research you're doing here?"

"It's not a research project that works if the buffalo get eaten!"

"We won't start eating them for another couple of months," Wolf said sarcastically. "I thought that job in Yellowstone only went to someone with a doctorate. I thought the preliminary work on the dissertation is what got you the job. They might have understood if Leonard pulled the rug out from under you, but are you sure it will still be there if you walk out?"

Buffy held his gaze. Then she looked beyond him at her buffalo, and her heart turned over to think of them butchered for the dinner table.

Wolf must have read her mind. "I'm a full-blooded Sioux. I come from a line of people who survived eating buffalo. My people believed buffalo served a noble purpose by giving their lives for us. We respected and even revered them for that. But we still ate them. It was survival. It was life. And you need to get your head out of the clouds and figure that out."

Wolf held her gaze with his black eyes. He waited, but Buffy didn't know for what, unless it was for her to give up everything she believed.

"I'm disappointed in you, girl. You're going to give up on the thing that could really save buffalo in this country. *That* is your dream. You're going to give up on a man who loves you. *That* is your future. I think you'll figure that all out someday. But by then, it'll be too late. Instead of being part of something, you'll be a spectator, a stuffed shirt intellectual sniffing at capitalism from some tenured position on a college campus."

His words cut her all the way to her heart. "I—I thought you liked me. I thought you respected me."

"I do like you, girl. I like you just fine. But respect? Well, now that's another thing altogether."

"And in order to earn your respect, I have to give up on what I believe is right and wrong? That's something you would respect?"

"I'm not asking you to do anything wrong, Buffy. You're an idealist, and that's a wonderful thing. But idealism is something you need to save for God. For your faith. When it comes to ranching, being a realist is as simple as life and death. Most people get around to being one after a while. It's called growing up, and it's high time you did it. Until you do," Wolf's tone softened to kindness, "your life is going to be an empty one."

Buffy almost caved. She almost asked him to tell her more about how he wanted to make a true buffalo commons. But stubbornness settled over her heart.

Wolf must have sensed it, because without another word, he headed for his truck and drove away.

❧

Yellowstone didn't want her.

The doctorate was a crucial piece of the puzzle they were putting together to research their herd. They needed her credentials. They didn't say she couldn't come. They said, "Finish the research. Write the dissertation."

"Aunt Buffy, take me out to look at the buffalo." Sally ran to the window a hundred times a day, but Buffy wouldn't let her go out.

Jeanie had been released from the hospital. The county attorney recommended probation, and both agreed to it. Jarvis, new to the area, had a history of psychological problems, and hostile and friendless, he'd let the local anger at the buffalo goad him into his first act of vandalism, cutting the fence and throwing the firecrackers. He hadn't meant it as anything more than a vicious prank. Then he'd met Jeanie, and the two of them had found soul mates in their resentment and talked each other into making a bigger strike at the herd.

His parents promised the court they'd get their troubled son into counseling, and they'd left the area. Jeanie had signed adoption papers for Sally, and she'd left without saying good-bye to anyone. Only after she was gone did Buffy realize that Jeanie had cleaned out her bank account.

Sally missed her mother, and Buffy would have done almost anything to make Sally happy. But not visiting the buffalo. She couldn't bear to see her big friends fattened for the grill. She saw Wyatt's truck come in and out several times a day, and why not? It was his ranch. He came to the door once and knocked, but she didn't answer.

She admitted after only a few hours that she had to stay and finish her project, but doing it made her sick. Three days had gone by, and still she couldn't go crawling to Wyatt, begging him for a job.

Long after Sally was asleep on the third day since she'd heard about Wyatt buying the Buffalo Commons, Buffy stared out the window and saw in the starlight that the herd had wandered close to the house. She let the peace buffalo always brought to her lure her to the corral. She sat on the top rung of the fence and stared.

"They're beautiful, aren't they?"

Buffy turned and saw Wyatt. "Where's your truck?" A stupid question but the first thing that came out of her mouth.

"Leonard bought me a new one. Yellow. It looks like a five-ton canary. I drove over here on field roads, inspecting the fence line. I left it behind Wolf's trailer so no one would see me and laugh."

"I thought Leonard was broke." Buffy frowned.

"I don't think broke means the same thing to billionaires as it does to us." Wyatt climbed the fence beside her and swung his legs around so he faced the herd. He didn't talk, and the silence, at first awkward, grew more companionable as the tranquility of the buffalo soaked into her soul.

"What do they say to you, Buffalo Gal? What was it that drew you to them to begin with?"

It was a question she'd been asked before, but she'd never told anyone the truth. "They're strong."

"That's it? Strong? Lots of animals are strong. Elephants, rhinos, Angus bulls."

Buffy smiled. "I was twelve years old, and I was on a field trip with my school. I'd had a fight with my father the night before over nothing and everything. He wanted to tell me every breath I could take. I talked on the phone too much. I chewed gum. Half my skirts were too short, and half were too long. My shirts were all either too baggy or too tight. If I wore makeup,

I was loose. If I left it off, I was ugly. It had nothing to do with me, and I know that now."

"How could it have nothing to do with you?"

"He was a man who liked to hurt people. Jeanie did everything he wanted as quickly as she could. I defied him every chance I got. Nothing either of us or our mother did made him stop yelling."

"I'm sorry he was unkind to you."

Buffy smiled. "Another apology."

"Just as useless as all the rest."

"Anyway, I was grounded for the thousandth time. He'd taken my lunch money away from me and made Mom send me a peanut butter sandwich for lunch, which to a twelve-year-old girl, at least to me, was humiliating. All the other kids had money, and the field trip included a stop at McDonald's. He'd banned me from talking on the phone for a month—no big deal as I didn't have any friends. But the man had a knack for cutting me to my heart. He made me feel ugly, but, well, he couldn't say I was stupid, not with my grades. He used that on Jeanie and Mom. He made me feel like a freak who was completely alone in the world."

Buffy heard Wyatt grinding his teeth and looked at his protective anger. "Stop that. You don't have to come charging to my rescue all the time."

Wyatt forced his shoulders to relax. Tears stung her eyes as she watched him try and respect her independence.

"Didn't you have any friends?" he asked.

Buffy turned from Wyatt to watch the buffalo. "Not really. I was two years younger than my classmates, in the same grade as Jeanie, which made her feel stupid, which she isn't. But because she was really popular, her hostility rubbed off on the other kids."

"So where does the buffalo come in?"

"We went to a natural history museum, and I wandered away from the group to bask in self-pity. I found an 'Animals of the Prairie Exhibit.'"

"And there was the buffalo," Wyatt said, nodding.

"A lot of the animals had little groups. You know. A doe, a buck, and a fawn. A wolf and his mate and their pups. There was even an opossum with its babies hanging from its tail. It was all so perfect, all these families. And there stood that buffalo. I guess the museum didn't have space or money for a family of them. There was just one. Alone, like me. I stared at that buffalo, into its black glass eyes, for what seemed like hours. It was an experience I really can't describe, Wyatt."

She looked at him. He was completely open to her, letting her talk, absorbing her words. Something her father was incapable of. She wished so much that he could understand.

"God was with me there in that museum. I looked at that strong animal standing alone." Tears burned her eyes, and her voice broke. "God told me I was going to have stand alone for a while."

Wyatt slid a little closer to her on that sturdy railing and took her hand.

"But He said it, so I could do it. He'd be with me, loving me. I will always believe in God without reservation because of that moment. It was absolute and true and undeniable. God has helped me through hard times, when my father seemed determined to break me. God has led me to the right people to encourage me. Did you know I graduated from high school when I was sixteen?"

"Wow."

"Yeah, and I already had two years of college behind me because of dual-credit courses the high school helped me find. I graduated from vet school when I was twenty."

"Man, our kids are gonna be smart, unless I drag down the

average." Wyatt must not have been very worried about their kids, because he rested his arm around her shoulders. "And now you're free of your family, but you don't know how to quit being alone."

"And the buffalo I love is going to be reduced to a commodity."

Wyatt pulled her closer. "Tell me what to do. I can't afford to keep these buffalo for you as a toy. If I could, I would. I know how horrified you were at the thought of them being turned into dog food. I thought I came up with a good plan that night. When I said I was going to buy the land, I meant for us and the buffalo. But you didn't even give me a chance to explain. And then I got so mad I didn't want to explain. You were so ready to believe I'd stab you in the back. What kind of love is that? What kind of marriage could we have if you did that all the time?"

"I guess I was ready to be betrayed. I think I was expecting it."

"Well, quit expecting it from me." He looked down at her and blocked out the whole world. "I'll never betray you. I love you. Tell me. I'm listening. Give me a way to save these guys. Tourism? I've thought of that. I don't know how many people will come all the way out here, but we can try. Mt. Rushmore's not that far away. We could draw a few people in. Supplying wild animal parks? We can do that for as many of them as we can sell. I'll let you take charge of all that. We'll save as many as we can, and maybe, once the herd is smaller, we can save them all. But for right now, we both know it's not going to be enough."

Buffy nodded and leaned her head against Wyatt's shoulder. So strong. So alone because she wasn't with him. "I've spent my whole life studying buffalo. I've researched their history, their genetics, their health, and how money is made from them."

"You'd be the perfect person to run this business."

"And the ones I couldn't save would have to die."

"Yes," Wyatt said without flinching. "It's not a perfect solution, but you know Yellowstone sells off part of its herd for meat. Leonard would have had to start doing it. You have to cull the herd somehow, or they overgraze the range and ruin the prairie grass and die of starvation."

"I've thought about it for years." Tears stung Buffy's eyes. "I've thought about it until I've got brain fatigue from thinking about it."

"You can't turn South Dakota into a buffalo commons. There are nearly a million people in this state. There's no natural barrier between here and Denver. It's impossible to move Denver. You know that."

Buffy nodded. "I know that."

"So tell Yellowstone to get themselves another girl. Stay here and finish your dissertation and be the most overeducated woman to ever hitch herself to a country boy with a high school diploma."

"I feel like I'm betraying them, Wyatt. Just like I've been betrayed."

"You're not. You're saving them. You'll be the woman who turned a novelty into a thriving breed. Stay here with me." He lowered his head and kissed her gently. "Be my Buffalo Gal."

He kissed her again.

Buffy let herself sink into the kiss. . .and her future.

At last she turned and studied the herd. Her friends. She said a prayer under her breath, "God, there is no other way." She was asking for forgiveness, and as simply as that, she knew God didn't think she needed it.

She sat still and felt Wyatt's tension and hope. And his love. "You're my future, Wyatt. You and Sally and the boys."

"And buffalo. You were called to care for them. I won't ever make you give that up."

"What if we can't make it pay?"

Wyatt hesitated. "Wolf is as passionate about these buff as you. He's not just hoping. He's done a lot of research. He thinks it'll work."

"If we can't afford to keep them, can I at least have one as a pet?"

Wyatt smiled in the moonlight; then he laughed. "It's a deal. And not just one. We'll make sure it's at least a family."

They sat together in the dark, with the buffalo. It had always been the time they were best together.

She turned away from the herd. "We can make it work."

"Is that a yes?"

Buffy rested her hand on his cheek and felt his strength. "That's a yes."

"No more standing alone," Wyatt added. "From now on, you're not a buffalo. You're that mama possum with babies hanging from her tail."

"Just how many children do you want to have?" Buffy asked suspiciously.

"How's seven sound?" Wyatt gave her a quick kiss on the nose.

"Seven?" Buffy slapped his arm, but there wasn't any force behind it.

"Well, we've got three already."

Buffy nodded. "That's a good start."

"This weekend—five days from now—we're getting married."

"There you go, being domineering again."

Wyatt gave her an unrepentant grin. "Let's go tell Sally and the boys."

"No, Sally's asleep." Buffy pointed at the baby monitor sitting beside her on the fence. "And so are the boys and Anna. Let's sit here awhile longer. I want to think among my buffalo."

So they sat, and she thought, but not for long.

God had told her she'd have to stand alone for a while. She'd done it. It had been hard, but it had forged her into the woman she wanted to be.

But the time was past. Now she'd stand with Wyatt.

She wasn't alone anymore.

epilogue

Buffy Lange became Ally Shaw, standing in front of a preacher, with a buffalo herd munching grass at her back.

Sally perched on Wyatt's shoulders through the ceremony. Cody and Colt only tried to shoot each other twice while the pastor was talking.

Wolf stood up with both of them, because although he refused to be a bridesmaid, he said it was disloyal to pick Wyatt over Buffy.

The S Bar B Ranch—Shaw Buffalo Ranch—was born.

A Letter To Our Readers

Dear Reader:
In order that we might better contribute to your reading enjoyment, we would appreciate your taking a few minutes to respond to the following questions. We welcome your comments and read each form and letter we receive. When completed, please return to the following:

Fiction Editor
Heartsong Presents
PO Box 719
Uhrichsville, Ohio 44683

1. Did you enjoy reading *Buffalo Gal* by Mary Connealy?
   ❑ Very much! I would like to see more books by this author!
   ❑ Moderately. I would have enjoyed it more if

   _____
   _____
   _____

2. Are you a member of **Heartsong Presents**? ❑ Yes ❑ No
   If no, where did you purchase this book? _____
   _____

3. How would you rate, on a scale from 1 (poor) to 5 (superior),
   the cover design? _____

4. On a scale from 1 (poor) to 10 (superior), please rate the
   following elements.

   ____ Heroine   ____ Plot
   ____ Hero   ____ Inspirational theme
   ____ Setting   ____ Secondary characters

5. These characters were special because? _____

   _____

   _____

6. How has this book inspired your life? _____

   _____

   _____

7. What settings would you like to see covered in future
   Heartsong Presents books? _____

   _____

   _____

8. What are some inspirational themes you would like to see
   treated in future books? _____

   _____

   _____

9. Would you be interested in reading other **Heartsong
   Presents** titles? ❑ Yes ❑ No

10. Please check your age range:
       ❑ Under 18   ❑ 18-24
       ❑ 25-34   ❑ 35-45
       ❑ 46-55   ❑ Over 55

Name _____

Occupation _____

Address _____

City, State, Zip_____

MARY CONNEALY

Schoolmarm Grace Calhoun has her work cut out for her with the Reeves boys—five malicious monsters of mayhem who are making her life miserable. Things couldn't get any worse. . .or could they?

Historical, paperback, 288 pages, 5³⁄₁₆" x 8"

Hearts♥ng

HEARTSONG PRESENTS TITLES AVAILABLE NOW:

Presents

Great Inspirational Romance at a Great Price!

Heartsong Presents books are inspirational romances in
contemporary and historical settings, designed to give you an
enjoyable, spirit-lifting reading experience. You can choose
wonderfully written titles from some of today's best authors like
Wanda E. Brunstetter, Mary Connealy, Susan Page Davis,
Cathy Marie Hake, Joyce Livingston, and many others.

When ordering quantities less than twelve, above titles are $2.97 each.
Not all titles may be available at time of order.